Praise for the
Bequia Perspectives N

.... murder and intrigue on a Caribbean island paradise ... I have seldom read a crime novel that captivates so well through the 'personality' of the setting as well as the masterful sculpting of the main characters... having lived for a time in an island environment, I recognise the illumination of each individual, and their unique place in this idyllic community ... terrific and satisfying read!

~ Seumas Gallacher, author of the Jack Calder crime-thrillers

I have read hundreds of mysteries in my life. I am drawn to them like a big galumphing fly is drawn to flypaper. Some are hard-boiled; others are softer in tone, like a warm summer day, more drifting and inconsistent. Susan Toy has written a charming hybrid; part travelogue, part mystery. This is proudly displayed on the back cover and is, by my reckoning, very accurate. She has assembled a representative cast of Bequian characters, expats of all sorts and a passel of locals, that we might well expect to meet again. We do want to meet them and find out more about their interesting Island.

~ Bill Engleson, author of *Like a Child to Home*

As winter approaches here in Canada, I like the opportunity to armchair travel to warmer climes even if there is a murder or two in the making. What do we know about Bequia? Not very much. We know much about its neighbouring island Mustique, hangout of the rich and famous. However, that is 10 miles away and Bequia is relatively unknown. Winston Churchill visited it once, and Anthony Eden lived there for a couple of years in the 1950's. Bequia is barely 7 square miles and has a population of around 6000. If a murder takes place in an island that size, it's possible that you know the culprit ... a good setup for a murder mystery.

~ Timothy L. Phillips, author of *My Camino Walk: A Way to Healing*

... you may also enjoy the other layer of these novels: the story of Bequia itself. By interspersing the crime plot with an in-depth, factual description of the island, Susan Toy lets you inhale its salty air, see its flamboyant colors and taste its flavors. She takes you to an exciting voyage through its history, geography, climate, to demographics, culture and mentality, so that you can feel the pulse of Bequia.

~ Librarian comment, Calgary Public Library

Also by Susan M. Toy

One Woman's Island

That Last Summer

Island in the Clouds

the

a *Bequia Perspectives* novel

by Susan M. Toy

IslandCatEditions
Calgary ~ Bequia

Published worldwide by

IslandCatEditions

ISBN print 978-1-927950-12-8
ISBN mobi 978-0-9879385-1-0
ISBN ePub 978-0-9879385-0-3

DISCLAIMER: This is a work of fiction. The characters do not exist, except in the mind of the author. Any resemblance to persons, living or dead, is purely coincidental.

Original Cover design: Jenny Ryan
Editor: Rachel Small, Faultless Finish Editing
2nd Edition cover and interior redesign: Human Powered Design
Cover and author photos: Dennis Ference

IslandCatEditions – susanmtoy@gmail.com

This book is dedicated to the memory of my parents who never saw Bequia.

Look at all those boats!

Prologue

Pronounced BECK-way, the name is a Carib Indian word meaning "island in the clouds." This description of Bequia holds even today—when flying from Barbados, you can't see the island at all until your last few moments in the air, because it is nestled in clouds. In their day, centuries ago, the Caribs didn't have the benefit of an air approach, so Bequia must have been hidden when they first paddled towards the island, making their approach in dugout canoes.

The first time I saw Bequia was from the ferryboat—still the best way to arrive. Nothing compares to the view when rounding the headland as you enter Admiralty Bay that includes West Cay, Moonhole and the entire southwest end of the island in the distance. As the leeward coast unfolds, first Lower Bay then Princess Margaret beaches come into view. Admiralty Bay's waters are dotted with sailboats of all types and lengths bobbing in the ferry's wake. Oftentimes you might also see a few large working boats and maybe a small cruise ship or two moored further out where it's deep. The ferry wharf at Port Elizabeth, the island's heart, is surrounded on three sides, like a natural amphitheatre, with lush, tropical-green hills dotted by colourful houses of varying sizes.

You can read the guidebooks for the facts: Bequia is located in the south-eastern Caribbean; the total land area is seven square miles; it's home to an interesting mix of six thousand or so, both locals and foreigners. Nine miles south of St. Vincent, Bequia is first in the string of the Grenadines, the southern islands trailing off like a kite's tail. It's also right next door to Mustique—the grown-up and more sophisticated older sister—a celebrated and world-renowned island habitat of the rich and famous. Instead, Bequia has always acted as a magnet for well-travelled and often down-at-heel sailors. And, unlike Mustique, it has no snob appeal; most people come to Bequia because they like the island, not because it's a place where spending large rolls of cash makes them look important.

The entire country of St. Vincent and the Grenadines was a late bloomer in a competitive tourism industry that, even now, hasn't developed into anything like St. Lucia, Barbados and Grenada, the better-known neighbouring Windward Islands. The relevant authorities say that what's kept this from happening is a lack of direct jet service from North America and Europe. So the country remains somewhat unknown, more closely resembling the old Caribbean of about thirty years ago.

Yet Bequia, unlike the rest of the country, has always enjoyed a thriving business with foreigners, in spite of its lack of air connections—or, as the expat community believes, due to that lack. Smitten visitors return, year after year, because the island remains undiscovered by the vast majority of sun-seeking all-inclusive tourists. For decades, excellent yachting conditions have attracted savvy travellers—not mere tourists—and those who are bent on finding an out-of-the-way destination that promises more relaxation, less shopping, fewer expensive restaurants, and no night clubs or chain hotels at all, unlike what is promoted on the bigger and better-known islands in the neighbourhood.

What guidebooks can't ever describe, though, is the strong affection, this warm glow, that everyone seems to develop for Bequia, even after their first visit. There's a certain *je ne sais quoi*, almost like a possessiveness of place, beckoning visitors to return countless times, until they feel compelled to put down stakes and become a permanent part of it. Many repeat visitors are eager to part with a life's savings to buy land and build holiday houses; some even pack in lives back home altogether, moving into the community forever and ever, or until their money runs out, or Bequia loses her charm.

Like them, I too have a love for this island that I can't quite define.

When you question others as to why they're so attached, they answer that it's because of the wonderful local people. Some will also try to tell you, when they hear my story, that I've got it all wrong and they will accuse me of carrying around a too-negative attitude about the island and its people. Yet their experiences aren't mine, and I don't mind saying I think I have a better sense of the place than they do; after all, I've lived here year-round, so I've seen both high and low seasons, the good, and the downright nastiness of the place and its people.

I should also mention that, unlike other expats, for me there was no choice; I had to escape to Bequia. But I'll get to that later. There's more you need to know before you start judging me.

After living full-time on this island for a couple of years, running my own business, dealing with the locals during prosperous as well as lean times, I've come to realize that Bequia people are no better, and no worse, than people anywhere else in the world. My own experience has been the same as for most expat permanent residents and somewhat different from that of short-term tourists. I've been here long enough that I tend to see the island for what it is, warts and all, without the shading of rose-coloured sunglasses. As in the rest of the outside world, unsavoury characters do live here and unfortunate things can happen. Bequia is not always paradise—far from it, sometimes.

St. Vincent and the Grenadines is, after all, the third world. Okay, the government likes to call this the "developing world," but it carries a third-world mentality, a country always dependent on foreign aid and an ever-dwindling banana market. Added to that, what remains of trade in bananas has received modest news coverage for experiencing a quick, but for the most part silent, death thanks to the WTO ruling against Windward Islands' exports in favour of US-backed Central American produce. So the writing is on the wall for this entire area of the East Caribbean. Unemployment isn't just continuing at crippling high levels: it may be worsening. The resulting poverty remains a major problem for the population of this country as a whole, and no government has ever figured out a solution. I believe no politician *wants* to solve these problems, because their ability to hold on to power is a direct result of keeping the populace heads-down, buried in the country's sandy beaches. But politics is another story about this place that needs to be told elsewhere, and on its own.

All this poverty-level living helps to further widen the gap between locals and, by comparison, us wealthy foreigners (although I would never consider myself wealthy by North American standards), leading to higher expectations among some who think we foreigners, and our money, will alleviate most of the country's problems. Now, I'm not saying this is the case with all locals. Many I know are good, honest people. But I've also had run-ins with those who try to take advantage—people who expect me to "sponsor" them (their way of asking for a simple monetary handout), or hire them as employees, although they're not prepared to actually *work* to earn money. That's happened enough times to sour my attitude. So I try to keep the local population at arm's length, other than those few people I employ—the very few I've found who do want to work.

Things don't always run as smoothly, either, as we foreigners think they should. In fact, sometimes everything is so back-asswards as to be infuriating—like my experiences dealing with the police, for instance. You'll hear about that later. And don't ever try reasoning with a customs agent, or anyone else wearing an official uniform, even the nurses, for that matter. Everything has a way of getting done, though never with a tortoise-wins-the-race kind of determination, but rather through the intervention of Lady Luck with her eyes covered over, and always in its own time.

So Bequia is not a perfect island, and it's not a total paradise; this makes me wonder if such a place, a paradise, exists anywhere in this world. But in spite of all my negativity, there is still *something* about Bequia that makes it as close to paradise on earth as we can ever hope to find. And whatever that something is manages to strike a chord with almost everyone who visits this place. They hold fond memories of it for the rest of their lives. By learning to accept, or ignore, the bad stuff—anyone can enjoy the island and lead a comfortable life.

The weather is pretty good, aside from the occasional threat of a hurricane. There are beautiful and somewhat deserted beaches that remain empty most of the year, even during the height of tourist season. And there's always a relaxed, casual atmosphere that welcomes anyone. It doesn't matter who they are, whether they have money or not, or what they did during previous lives—both successful and infamous are accepted. No one on Bequia ever cares about the reasons why someone may have washed up on the island's shores.

For people within the expat community, like my friends Doc, Melanie, Al, Suzie and Mike, what brought each of us to Bequia and what prevents us from leaving has always been a great topic of conversation. The one consensus is that we can't quite put a finger on that elusive element. If nothing else, and perhaps out of boredom, the entire concept is a constant and inexhaustible topic whenever we get together. After all, there isn't much else by way of entertainment to pass the time.

Attracting such a diverse group of foreigners as it does, Bequia also offers a safe, remote haven to people needing to run away, or even escape, from the outside world for a while. People like me, for instance . . .

Now Bequia has had its share of bogus German barons and questionable Italian countesses—people backed by their own braggadocio, chutzpah, and vivid imaginations. We've seen millionaires of both the self-made and trust-fund varieties come and go, plenty of retirees, and an inordinate number of middle-aged women looking for a last promise of love in the arms of a local boy more than half their age. They just end up making fools of themselves.

What I'm getting at is that this place attracts all kinds, and everyone has a story. Sometimes the stories we hear even turn out to be true—although, on Bequia, we're reminded by the locals that we should believe nothing of what we hear and only half of what we see. People have been known to arrive and spread the most outrageous fantasies about themselves, talking the "big talk" that they plan to develop an island-saving business and employ many, or offer to turn the locals' lives around by sponsoring entire families with money for education or medical trips abroad. Yet no one on the island ever realizes it's all a hoax until long after the culprits have left, having caused certain irreparable damage and managing to swamp many, many people in their wake. A group of European investors did just that by pulling the plug on their promised development soon after clearing the land, by which time the locals had already been duped into accepting that a concocted get-rich-quick scheme would be the island's salvation. All that experience did was make the hoodwinked-locals wary and the rest of us foreigners who remained look bad. But I can say, in all honesty, that neither my friends nor I have ever tried to cheat anyone. We're all happy not to bother, or be bothered by, anyone. We just want to live quiet and private lives.

You want to hear the truth about Bequia? Well, I'll tell you what happened to me. I guarantee what I am about to tell you is true. But then, you have no other choice than to believe what I say, do you?

Chapter One

Racing down the stone path towards the pool, I cursed that last rum and Coke of the previous night. It was just 7:00 a.m., Monday, the busiest day of my week, but I should have been there forty-five minutes earlier. That drink, that last one, was responsible for making me sleep late and would punish me further as I fell behind schedule for the rest of the day.

Unlocking the garden shed door, I hauled out the cleaning equipment and dragged it across the patio. I stopped by the edge of the pool and stood, wavering, looking down, trying to focus my eyes in the sharp sunlight. I'd forgotten to pick up my shades in the rush to leave home. I blinked hard; the rippling reflection in the water made me cringe. I did look as bad as I felt; I needed a shave and hadn't even had time to comb what hair I still had. But then, out of the corner of one eye, something drew my attention away from that ugly visage. I turned my head, blinking against the morning sun's brilliant glint off the water, and focused on an object that looked even worse than I did—a body floating face down at the far end of the pool. A woman's body; a naked woman's body.

"Oh, shit!" I slapped my forehead with the palm of my hand. My immediate, selfish reaction was that this was going to further screw up my day. Not to mention throw off the pool's pH balance.

Then my hangover fog began to lift as the gravity of the situation sank in. I rubbed both fists into my eyes and peered again. Was it just a rum-induced pink elephant? No, the body was still there and I could feel the panic rising. I watched for a moment, trying to calm myself, to clear my thinking, gulping air like a fish out of water in an attempt to keep a sudden bilious eruption in the pit of my stomach from moving up any higher. A slight breeze caused a noticeable ripple on the water's surface, just enough to make the body drift in a repetitive bump against the pool's rim. Otherwise, there was no movement at all—no bubbles, anyway, and no point jumping in to save her. She was already dead.

After two years managing foreigners' properties on the island of Bequia, I'd fished my share of bodies out of pools—all rodent and insect, though, never human.

Now, I like naked women as much as the next guy, but a dead naked woman is another matter. Floating face down, her backside was all I could see. So, even if I had known her, I wasn't able to say who she was, having had little opportunity to examine too many women's backsides on this island.

My effort at keeping that bile at bay was becoming futile. I needed to move, but didn't want to pull her out just to satisfy morbid curiosity. She was in good physical shape, though—apart from the fact that she was floating face down. There were no tan lines and her skin was still fish-belly white. In all likelihood she'd just arrived, one of any number of foreigners, almost all tourists, attracted to this tropical paradise for its sun, fun, and rum.

But why did she have to wind up in one of the pools I managed? And why this day of all days? I already had enough problems in my life as it was. I didn't need another.

Maybe I'd watched too much TV while growing up, but all those detective shows helped me decide I shouldn't disturb the body. I left it floating and trudged back up the hill to the house, thinking my next best plan would be to phone the police.

The owner was off-island, so the house had been empty for about a month. I fumbled in my pocket for the key, unlocked the kitchen door, and pushed it open.

First things first, though, I thought, and headed straight for the liquor cabinet. Times like this call for straight scotch, no rocks. Now, don't get me wrong: I'm not an alcoholic, and I'm not in the habit of pilfering from my clients' private supplies. But, considering the circumstances, this particular owner wouldn't mind if I helped myself to his best, a twenty-year-old Lagavulin, for medicinal purposes only, mind you. I had a second quick shot to steady my nerves and further delay the pounding headache that was already beginning to gather behind my eyes. Then I got down to business.

Since there isn't a general 9-1-1 emergency number for Bequia, I had to contact the authorities one at a time. Knowing it would take the local police a while to arrive at the scene anyway, I called the doctor first. Besides, he's my friend and, along with his wife, a notorious before-the-crack-of-dawn riser. Even though they'd been drinking with me the previous night, neither would be suffering from a similar hangover—they're both so self-controlled it makes me sick without the aid of alcohol.

"Misery loves company," I said aloud as their phone began ringing.

Doc answered with a business-like "Dr. Halliday."

Dave, a fellow Canadian, is the one medical doctor on Bequia. His friends call him Doc, and he and his wife have been happy campers on the island for about ten years, after having had their fill, on an equal basis, of cold Canadian winters and a bureaucratic health care system. At least on Bequia, even with limited resources, he can practice medicine the way he was trained, without having to jump through government hoops, completing endless forms, treating patients as statistics. He would have made a great deal more money had he stayed in Canada, but financial reward has never been important to either of the Hallidays.

"Doc, I've got a big problem here at The Clouds. You know, Wilson's place in Hope?" I was trying to be casual, attempting to cover my panic, which began rising again like fluids in a volcanic magma chamber, constricting my throat while I was speaking. "C-could you come over as soon as possible? There's what you might call a foreign object floating in the pool. A dead foreign object."

"Geoff, are you sure you're not seeing things?" Doc said, calm, even adding a chuckle. "I'm surprised *you're* still alive this morning considering what you put back last night."

I didn't laugh. His reminder made me shudder. My own memory of my behaviour the night before was still a little sketchy, but I didn't need it spelled out. "This is serious. I need you to have a look at her."

"A woman?" All humour left his voice. "Do you know who she is? Did you try to resuscitate her?"

"No to both. I left her in the pool. She's definitely dead. But I thought I shouldn't touch anything anyway, until someone else had a chance to look. Can you come over right now? I'll call the police. Maybe they'll even understand the urgency. Then we can all stand around and have a look together."

Doc would have caught my sarcasm but, remaining serious, said, "I'll be on my way in a few minutes. Mel wants to talk to you."

Before I had a chance to thank him, I heard Doc describe for Melanie what I'd found. She was on the line in a nanosecond.

"Are you all right, Geoff?"

"Sure, except now this is beginning to sink in. It's not every day I find someone dead first thing in the morning. Or any time, for that matter, especially on this island." I shuddered. The numbing effects of that scotch were already beginning to wear off.

"Do you know who she is?"

"I can't tell, other than that she's white. The body is face down. I don't want to move her before Doc gets here."

"I understand. Poor you! Is there anything I can do to help?" Melanie is such a brick. No matter what, we can always depend on her to provide calming good sense, with times of crisis being her particular specialty.

"Now that you mention it, Mel, would you mind picking up the Brethren? Drive them over to the Collins' place for me?" Knowing the guys as I do, the two Rastafarian gardeners I employ would be standing by the roadside thinking it was time to roll a spliff, if it looked as though work was cancelled. After the morning's events, I was tempted to join them, just to escape what I suspected would become a mess of a day.

"Okay. Where and when?"

Somewhat relieved, I began to relax. "They'll be expecting me at seven thirty by the cemetery road. Once you get them out to Spring, they'll know what to do. Tell them we'll meet later this morning, as soon as I can get away from here."

"Sure, that's no problem. Do you want me to call Angie?" I got the impression Melanie was writing down my instructions. Good old Mel—ever the organized, dependable, nice Canadian.

"No, don't disturb her. She's probably still asleep. I'll drop by the house before I go out to the Collins' place and explain what's up. Thanks, Mel."

"Anytime, Geoff, although let's hope it's the last time something like this happens. Dave's walking out the door. He should be there in ten minutes."

After hanging up, I resisted the urge to pour another shot of scotch. It was time to try contacting the police.

When I dialled the station number I counted fifteen rings before hanging up. On the second try the line was busy. I redialled several times, becoming more and more frustrated at not getting through. Then, at last, I heard a disinterested voice, but at least it was human and not the answering machine I'd half been expecting to hear next. Someone on the other end had seemed bent on avoiding my repeated calls—and any work those calls might bring the police. Doc arrived just as Corporal Something-or-Other answered; his dialect was so thick I couldn't understand him. I didn't want to appear stupid by asking him to repeat his name. After listening without comment, or even any sound of breathing, to my long and detailed explanation of the discovery and directions for finding the house, the corporal assured me they would have someone on the scene—as soon as their one vehicle returned from the other side of the island. It was, he said, changing shifts from the Paget Farm Police Station to the one in Port Elizabeth. Which meant someone might arrive within a matter of hours—that is, if the corporal remembered to tell anyone of my call in the first place.

I stared at the handset in disbelief and hung up, shaking my head as Doc walked through the door. "Man, this local 'can't do' attitude really pisses me off!"

Doc shrugged his shoulders. "What can you expect? It's the island way. The woman's already dead so, as far as the police are concerned, there's no need to rush. I'm not convinced they would, even if you'd told them she was still alive, bleeding, and calling for help. We all know these police are just trained at a minimum level to shine their shoes and buttons, to march in a straight line. They don't have any experience dealing with actual emergencies."

"True, but then how many real emergencies have there been to give them any practice?"

"You have a point." Doc said, nodding and adding, "Oh, and a piece of advice—the next time you have an emergency, simply tune in to Channel 68 on your VHF radio and broadcast 'Any Taxi!'"

These were pre cell-phone times. Nowadays, everyone—regardless of whether they earn money—owns a mobile.

"You'll get an immediate response from about ten drivers, and one may actually inform the police of your distress call. Some of them will even come out to lend a hand and not just to gawk and gossip."

"Doc, I do think you've lived on this island too long. You're beginning to sound as cynical as me," I said, laughing. He was usually a glass-half-full kind of guy.

"Not cynical." He elbowed me in the ribs. "Practical. I know Bequia's limitations and decided long ago to work around them rather than let them frustrate me. No point in kicking yourself in the butt over things you can't change, is there? Now, show me your dead woman. You look awful yourself, by the way," he said, moving towards the door.

"Gee, thanks, pal. And she's not 'my' dead woman. As far as I know, I've never even met her. But then I've only seen her back. Let's go." I passed him on my way out of the kitchen and took a couple of steps down the path to the pool.

Hesitating behind me, he said, "I hope you didn't touch anything in there. I can't help noticing you smell like a distillery. We don't want the police getting the wrong impression."

Good old Doc. Always sensible, just like his wife.

I stopped and, turning to face him, held up my hand. "Look, I'm not drunk now. It's just a hangover. I had a single shot of scotch earlier—one, uno—to brace myself after the shock of finding a dead body. You know, hair of the dog?" Doc smirked. "Okay, I had two shots. But I doubt anyone else has been in the house because I have the one key. There won't be any clues to disturb, anyway." I paused, nodding at him. "Good advice though, Doc, about not touching anything. We'll both have a look through the rest of the house later, okay? Just to see if anyone has broken in. Come on, the pool is down this way." I turned back around and we continued.

By that time, it was seven-thirty, but the day was promising to become another scorcher—hot and humid like the Toronto summer nights of my childhood. The sky was already an eye-piercing, clear blue. The middle of July, the time when all this took place, is the beginning of hurricane season. On Bequia, there's seldom any serious weather until September, though, so July and August can often be hot, dry months; the cooling trade winds the island enjoys throughout the rest of the year are scarce.

And that summer was no exception. We'd been experiencing a drier spell than usual and while the religious prayed for relieving rain the rest of us checked satellite maps, hoping for any indication that a reprieve, in the form of a tropical wave, was on its way from Africa. On Bequia, water is collected in cisterns from rainfall rather than accessing the water table with wells. That year, levels in many tanks were either running low or already being replenished by a company trucking in potable water. We were long overdue for a good torrential downpour.

The problem with the tropics is the weather is always, well, tropical, with no real change to break the monotony. Those who think they need the variety of four distinct seasons might not find that appealing, but, for the most part, I must say I do appreciate living here year-round, at least as far as the weather's concerned. I've become accustomed to the two seasons Bequia offers, rainy and dry, and I don't miss Canadian winters at all. Sometimes, though, my secret wish is for a good bracing snowstorm to surprise us, just for a simple change of pace, you understand. It could last for three hours and then all trace of it would have to melt away. Lucky for the tourists escaping their own dreary climate, the weather gods have, so far, ignored me. Besides, driving the steep-graded roads on Bequia would be a real bitch if they were ever to ice over.

When Doc and I landed on the patio and looked down at the body in the pool, he asked, "So, what do you think? Suicide or murder?"

"I don't know. Hadn't thought of suicide at all. I just assumed she was murdered. Do people usually undress first when they commit suicide? Come to think of it, Marilyn Monroe was nude when they found her. But then, did she really commit suicide?"

"I think you're getting sidetracked."

"Right. So, where are her clothes, anyway?"

We both searched around the pool and patio area but found nothing.

"Well, if it was murder," Doc said, "she was probably drowned. I don't see any blood at all, in the water or on the patio. I wish the police would get here. I don't want to drag the body in until they've had a look themselves, but I hate to leave her floating like that."

Then he looked at me and added, "Oh, and a warning, my friend—be prepared to become prime suspect. You were first to find her, so you're the easiest person to charge. That would allow for a quick close to this case, making the police look good."

"Yeah, I know. That thought already crossed my mind. They wouldn't have to do any investigating at all if they could just handcuff and charge the nearest breathing person. But thanks." I paused a moment, thinking, then asked, "Hey, just a minute—why wouldn't you be considered a suspect? You're here too, aren't you?"

He puffed up with mock pride. "Ah, but I would never be charged for anything on Bequia due to my status, dear compatriot, of being the highly respected island doctor!" He laughed. "I have the power that comes with any position of authority among these people. Like the police, customs, immigration officials, even the guy who sits in the booth for Port Authority and picks his teeth all day, I'm untouchable, without blame. I just don't wear a uniform."

I rolled my eyes. He was beginning to sound like Sherlock Holmes instead of the doctor.

A car drove up behind the house at the entrance to the property—a Suzuki, by the sound of the sewing-machine-like engine. If it proved to be the lone island police vehicle, we were being rewarded with a record response time by Bequia's finest. Things were looking up. Doc and I climbed the path towards the house to meet them.

Doc was right. At best, the police investigation was cursory. No photographs were taken. In fact, all the police brought was a roll of yellow crime-scene tape, which they proceeded to wrap around everything. Their lackadaisical attitude kind of knocked me back. I had expected a bit more excitement from them, even if the police did have a bad rep on the island for never wanting to do any work. After all, this was a murder.

Also, as Doc forewarned, I was their prime suspect and would have been arrested, tried, and hanged by the end of that day had Doc not vouched for my innocence.

Once we were back at the pool, Sergeant Simmons took charge. He pointed at Doc, then me. "You could pull out de body," he said, in the disarming way Vincentians have of changing questions into direct statements and vice versa. But his was more than a simple request for help. I guessed he expected us to do all the work because they didn't want to get their uniforms wet.

"Should the body be moved yet? Aren't you going to take photos?" Knowing the answer would be no before I even asked, I looked over at Doc, shrugged my shoulders, then went to retrieve a grappling hook out of the shed. I grappled while Doc grabbed as the body reached the pool's edge. We hauled her out with delicate reverence, turning her over onto her back.

It took a few moments searching my memory banks before I could place the face. I was taken aback.

"Mrs. Wilson . . . "

She was the estranged wife of the owner of the house, that house—The Clouds. I'd met her once two years before, soon after arriving on Bequia for the first time myself, just as she was leaving.

"Sarah," Doc said after a moment, sucking in breath as he pronounced her name.

"You both knows she? You cans identify de body?" the sergeant said. This was one of those times when a question was an actual question.

"Well, not really. She was married to my client." I was bewildered more than anything. "I only met her once. I didn't know she was on-island."

"I knew *of* her," Doc said, correcting the sergeant. "She used to come here as a tourist, before this house was built. "But it's definitely Sarah." He exchanged a glance with me.

We'd heard the rumours, knew of her abrupt departure from the island after she became involved, and none-too-discreet about it either, with one of the local beach bums. The gossips had it that wife and hubby suffered through a bitter and messy divorce as a result. He retained ownership of their Bequia house in exchange for a generous cash settlement, along with her agreement never to set foot on the island again. It seemed she had not kept her side of the deal.

Although my client and I never discussed any of his past history, the island rumour-mongers were most times reliable, except when their eagerness overruled any accuracy. Small details were questionable and often a product of overactive imaginations.

"Look at this," Doc said. He stepped aside and pointed at a small bullet hole at the top of Sarah's left breast, a perfect shot at the heart. "She would have died instantly."

But it made me wonder why there wasn't any blood in the pool. I remained silent.

"Whoever de woman, you must finish up here. We has to gets back to de station," Sergeant Simmons said. He turned to the constable and ushered him over to the side of the patio to stand beside a spray of red bougainvillea.

Small grey thunderclouds seemed to be forming above Doc's head as he watched the men's backs. He snatched up his bag and wrenched it open. In a matter of minutes, he determined time of death to have been somewhere between nine the previous night and four in the morning.

"You cans be more exact?" the sergeant said.

"No." Doc's lips made the slightest movement when he replied. I could tell this policeman was getting under his skin, to the point where Doc was done with co-operating.

"And who de husband?"

"Ex-husband. He's American," I said, keeping it simple, just as Doc had. Any further details wouldn't have mattered to these police, anyway. Suffice it to say he was a white foreigner. They could understand that.

"Where he at now?"

A corporate lawyer in his mid-fifties, the owner of The Clouds lived in Boston. Mr. Wilson had always seemed like a good guy; I considered him a fair-minded businessman. As far as I was concerned, he could not have killed his ex-wife. Besides, he'd been off-island and was not due back again for another month. His was an ironclad alibi—even if he did have the most obvious motive.

"When I call him, I'll ask where he's been lately."

"Could you find something to cover Sarah?" Doc said to me. "I don't like leaving her out here, exposed like this." He glanced over at the two police, who were continuing to stare at Sarah's naked body.

"Sure." I walked back up to the house, relieved to get away from the whole scene for a few minutes. I pulled a sheet off one of the beds, went back to the patio, and handed it to Doc, who draped it over Sarah.

"I called for an ambulance before I left home. I'd better call again." Doc made a move towards the path.

"We goes to de house," Sergeant Simmons said, taking charge again. "We all goes." He pointed to include me. "We needs to looks inside."

I turned and, in silence, followed Doc, the police close in my wake. They were either afraid to be left alone with the body or were just curious to see inside one of these expensive, foreign-owned villas that dot Bequia. It might have been more productive had we all looked around the outside of the house first. I knew no one would have broken in. The Clouds is an American architect's idea of tropical design—in other words, big and opulent, with no eye to living within, or as part of, a natural outdoor setting. To begin with, the house is air-conditioned throughout. That alone forces a Fort Knox style, keeping all the expensive cool air inside the walls, and the hot and humid air out. There's just one key for two locking doors—a simple system that saves me having to juggle a chain of possibilities like I must at another house I manage. Even when this owner is in residence, the house remains enclosed, insular and unwelcoming, like it has something to hide. The Clouds is the exact opposite to what most foreigners choose to build on Bequia—open concept with wide doors leading out to large verandahs that take full advantage of sweeping views and tropical breezes. I prefer the latter style. This house didn't even have the benefit of a great view.

We entered the kitchen again. Doc was already on the phone, looking angry at whoever was on the other end. I led the police through so they could check out the adjoining living room and from there to an enclosed verandah. I hadn't been that far into the house earlier and so saw for the first time that two drinking glasses, both containing an amber liquid, were set out on a small table, two chairs placed on either side of it.

"These weren't here when I checked the house last week." I walked over to the table, bent down, and sniffed the contents of one glass. There was a familiar fragrance of the fine Scotch I'd consumed earlier with guilty gulps. Someone who shares my good taste, I thought.

"You check de doors?" the sergeant said, becoming officious, gesturing his order at me.

My lips thinned. I turned around and had a look at the other entry and all the windows that might have given an opportunity. There were no signs of a break-in that I could see.

I reported back to him, "Whoever was in here must have had a key. But, as far as I know, I'm the only person on the island who has one, or so the owner told me."

Wilson held the other key. Both locks were changed after the separation agreement had been reached. So, if Sarah had been in the house before she was murdered, she had to have gained entry with the help of a locksmith.

"I must calls de station," Simmons said, marching to the kitchen, leaving me with the uncommunicative constable, who seemed more interested in checking out the house contents than considering the job at hand.

I took another look around the room and the verandah, hoping to demonstrate how the constable might consider doing his job, but he continued studying the shelves, and all he said was, "I can has these books?"

I turned my back on him in silent disgust and followed the sergeant.

Simmons was on the phone when I joined him. He said, "We finish here, sir. We returns now."

Doc was standing off to the side of the kitchen, simmering in his anger by the look of it. I told him of our discovery and Doc just said, "Uh-huh." Then we all kept our mouths shut until we heard the distant sound of the ambulance siren a minute or two later.

The sergeant called, "Ollivierre!" The constable walked in from the living room with speed I hadn't thought him capable of possessing. Before they left the house, Simmons turned to me and said, "You must comes by de station later to answer more questions and make an official statement. De inspector tell me so."

I watched the two men shuffle up the path to the property's entrance.

More questions, I thought. How about any questions . . .

"Correct me if I'm wrong, Doc, but shouldn't they have stayed here with the body until it was collected?" I said, glad in any case that they were gone.

"I think it was making them too squeamish. The constable was turning a remarkable shade of green around the gills after I pointed out the bullet hole. I'll bet he's never encountered a dead body before, except maybe his dead auntie in a casket." Doc flashed a sadistic grin.

I glanced at him, wondering if, due to my initial reaction when I found the dead body, I was wearing a similar shade of green. This wasn't the first one I'd seen in my life, but the others had died of natural causes and been in coffins, decked out in their Sunday finest, not unlike the constable's auntie. Unless you're in the business, like Doc, few people ever actually see anyone who's died, let alone murder victims.

"Let's go inside. I suppose I should call Mr. Wilson and let him know what's happened."

While I was looking for the number, Doc went out to the enclosed verandah.

He shouted, "Hey, wasn't there still some scotch in these glasses when you found them?"

"Yeah, in both of them. Why?" I joined him to have a look.

"Well, I wouldn't be surprised if our constable helped himself to what was left." He nodded at the now-empty glasses. "But whoever drank it also touched and moved them, so any evidence is gone. That is, presuming the police were planning on coming back to dust for fingerprints."

In spite of his earlier resignation towards the way things sometimes don't seem to work on Bequia, Doc was sounding disgruntled, like the rest of the island population, over another lacklustre performance by the local police.

"I think you're being too hard, Doc. I have a feeling that particular constable wants to become a good cop." He threw me a disbelieving look, so I added with a wide grin, "Don't worry. I'm being facetious. But he does just need more experience. After all, it's not every day the police have an opportunity to investigate a murder on Bequia. Do you remember the last one we had here?"

"Long before you arrived."

"Right. So this young guy has probably never dealt with a violent death before. He looked green in more ways than one. His uniform still had that stiff-new appearance. But I think he wants to improve himself." I threw Doc a wink-wink-nudge-nudge look. "He asked if he could borrow a couple of the John Grisham novels from the bookshelf. Well, take them, was what he actually said. Maybe he's planning to do some research into policing and the law."

Doc said, laughing, "Well, that's true. Few police have any experience. The whole situation with them this morning has been funny, I suppose, in a bizarre way. It's sad about Mr. Wilson's ex, though."

That comment sobered us both. I went back into the kitchen, pulled the phone number list out of a drawer, and dialled Wilson's office.

When I got through, I told the receptionist it was an emergency, and she transferred the call to Wilson without ceremony.

Never having delivered such news before, I figured the direct approach was best. That's how I would have wanted to hear it. When he answered, I said, "Mr. Wilson. Hi, it's Geoff on Bequia. I'm afraid I have some bad news about your ex-wife." I explained my morning's experience.

There was a quick intake of breath. I waited as he exhaled in auditory slow motion.

"Mr. Wilson? Are you okay?"

"Yes, Geoff, I'll be all right. Thanks for calling." He was silent then. I waited for him to speak, but when he did, it seemed as though he was returning from a long distance. "I'm sorry, but I think I'm sort of in shock." There was another pause while Wilson composed himself. When he came back on the line, he sounded worse than I'd expected. Maybe my method had been too abrupt.

"I haven't spoken with Sarah in over six months. Haven't seen her at all for longer than that. I had no idea she was even on Bequia. You say you found her this morning?"

"Yes, just now. Well, awhile ago, to be honest. I waited until I thought you were in the office before calling," I lied. "The police have already been here, and the doctor."

He blurted out, "You may think this is crazy, Geoff, but I loved Sarah . . . still love her . . . I know there were stories about us, about our marriage. They weren't true. We weren't divorced, you know. She was still my wife. Our separation may have appeared to have been bitter, but we were amicable. I wasn't so naive as to think we could ever reconcile, but I love . . . loved her." He sighed, the breath catching in his throat.

"I'm sorry for your loss, Mr. Wilson," I said, uncomfortable, not knowing how to console him, or stop him from saying too much. Then, remembering the police would need to know if he had an alibi, I asked, "Were you in Boston all weekend?"

"Uh, yes . . . oh, I understand, Geoff. Please confirm with the police that I have not been to Bequia for at least a month."

"Okay. It did come up. I'll be sure they make a note of it."

"Thanks, Geoff. I'll book a flight and get to Bequia as soon as possible," he said, under control again, getting back to business. "I'll let you know when I expect to arrive. In the meantime, I would very much appreciate your help. You've always been capable handling everything else for me, and I know the police there can't be trusted to do their jobs. Will you ask around, see if you can find out who did this?"

"Uh, okay, Mr. Wilson." In one brief moment, I'd become more involved than I wanted, or could afford, to be. And that was irritating. Drawing attention to myself was the last thing I needed. But what could I say? The guy's wife had been murdered. He deserved answers.

Wilson said, "I had to deal with the Bequia police when we were robbed a few years ago. That was before I hired you. The investigative abilities of the police were a joke and they never did capture the thief. Chances were he was responsible for a number of other break-ins at that time, too, but the police couldn't connect the crimes. I doubt there's been any improvement."

"Well, from what I saw this morning, I have to agree with you."

"Geoff, if you hear anything at all that might explain what happened to Sarah, please call me right away. I'll give you my personal cell number so you can contact me at any time."

I wrote down the information.

"Okay. Let me know when you expect to arrive in Barbados. I'll make arrangements for the private charter service to fly you over."

"Thanks. I have to tie up a few things at the office first, so it may be a couple of days before I can get away. Oh, and one other thing," he said, speaking fast, as though leaving no room for refusal. "Would you mind organizing the cremation of Sarah's body, and then a burial service to be held soon after I arrive? It needn't be religious. Burial at sea might be . . . suitable. Sarah always loved the sea. We never had children, and there are no other relatives, so I'm her only next-of-kin." His voice was breaking again, making him sound like he was about to crack up altogether. "And since I'll be the only mourner, the service might as well be held on Bequia."

Well, investigating murders and organizing funerals were a little above and beyond our property management contract, and not what I'd expected would be part of my general duties when I first set up the business. But Wilson had always been a decent client and seemed like a nice enough guy. He paid on time and wasn't too demanding. As irritated as I was, he sounded upset and in need of my support and help, at least here on Bequia, so I couldn't turn down his requests, unusual as they were. What kind of a heel would that make me look like?

"Sure, no problem. I'll take care of it." I was relieved when he hung up.

Breaking bad news to anyone is always difficult, so I suppose I was lucky Wilson had taken my call like a man, all in all. The Wilsons' relationship had not been perfect, but he said he still loved her, so who was I to judge? I hadn't needed to hear him blubbering at the other end of the line, though. There was enough I had to do for the man as it was without having to act as his counsellor as well.

With that unpleasant chore finished, I went outside to search for Doc. The ambulance had arrived and he was down by the pool helping the attendants. Once Sarah's body was stowed, they drove off towards Port Elizabeth with the siren wailing the entire way. It's not often they get to use that siren, so they tend to make the most of it whenever there's a chance. Besides, there's no better way to alert the rest of the island to a recent disaster. Everyone on Bequia would soon know what had happened, anyway. News has a way of travelling fast, and bad news even faster.

"Hey, they took the sheet!" I said. "I need that back."

"I'll make sure to retrieve it for you when I go to the clinic."

"Thanks. Don't forget, I'm responsible for everything in the house. And Wilson tends to be kind of fussy about his things."

"Sorry. I forgot what a conscientious property manager you are," he said, snickering.

"Yeah, well, I seem to have picked up some new responsibilities on top of everything else I have on my plate." Hoping to delegate one of them, I asked, "So, Doc, tell me: has Melanie ever organized a funeral before?"

He thought for a moment, then said, "Not that I can recall, but I'm sure she'll do a remarkable job, especially if you want it catered." He laughed.

Everyone knows Doc's wife is the best cook on the island, and her forte is organizing lavish dinner parties. Thanks to Melanie, no one else eats quite as well as our small group of friends. We refer to her with affection as the "Martha Stewart of Bequia." But I'm pretty sure the other expat women envy her culinary and organizational skills. If the Pope ever chooses to visit, Melanie is the one person who will be capable of making all arrangements so that everything comes together without a hiccup.

"Wilson also asked me to do some investigative work into Sarah's murder. I haven't got a clue where to begin."

"Well, don't look at me for answers. I didn't even know these people. They stuck with their own friends whenever they came here. In any case, I always found him to be rather secretive after she left. At least, he kept pretty much to himself, from what everyone has told me. I'll ask Mel. See if she knows anything more about them."

"Thanks. That's a start, at least. Wilson really wanted to yak. He told me way more than I needed to know."

"Cut the guy some slack. You just told him his ex-wife was murdered."

"Oh, sorry, but not ex, as it turns out. He said they never divorced. Seems that the Bequia gossips may have imagined a few of the stories about the Wilsons that have been circulating. I wonder what else they got wrong." Then I glanced at my watch. "Whoa! Look at the time. I've got a lot to do, besides reporting in at the police station now as well."

"Me too. I'm scheduled to work at the clinic in Paget Farm this morning. How about we meet later today at my house for drinks? I'll ask Al and Suzie, and Mike, too. Bring Angie."

"She has to work this evening, but we could come over for a sundowner. She doesn't need to be at the hotel until eight. And you're right. One of our friends might have an idea as to what happened here and who's responsible. Thanks, Doc. And, hey, thanks for all your help. See ya later."

Without answering, Doc turned and gave me a quick back-handed wave while walking up the steps to his car. I watched until he'd driven away. Then I went back down to the patio.

Standing in front of the shed for a moment, I opened my mouth wide and screamed, "Aw, hell!" at the top of my lungs, letting loose with a punch to the aluminum wall. I winced as I pulled my fist back, shaking out the pain. Rather than relieving my anger, all I'd managed to do was increase it, except now I was also angry at my own stupidity.

I got down to work and cleaned the pool, dropping an extra chlorine tablet into the skimmer, just in case. I locked up the house then drove to the Collins' place to check up on the Brethren. It was getting late, so I would make it a quick stop there. I was anxious to get back home and tell Angie all my news.

Chapter Two

I never dreamed of moving to Bequia.

I'm Canadian, late thirties, divorced. The ex rediscovered her childhood sweetheart and walked out, taking along a hefty alimony. I could also tell you I'm tall, dark, and handsome, but let's not worry about details.

A petroleum geologist by trade, I was on the board of directors of a junior oil company in Calgary before leaving Canada. I won't mention the name, but you'd recognize it in an instant because, two years ago, there was a major scandal. I had to disappear in order to ensure the company's future. I originally founded it with three buddies, guys I'd known since school days. We were young, cocky, and invincible, with a sense of entitlement, and we thought we were on our way to the top after taking the company public to raise capital for exploration drilling. I didn't come up with the idea to, let's say, "enhance" some exploration results and benefit from inside information, but the entire board, made up of my cohorts, was in agreement when we made our move. We believed it was time to receive our big, and well-deserved, payoff and thought this was the quickest route to success.

At our last secret board meeting, the one item on the agenda upon which we didn't agree, however, was that I would be the fall guy, the company scapegoat who, in the end, would shoulder the entire blame if our scam was ever revealed. It did take the rest of my friends some time to convince me; I was reluctant to succumb to their scheme. But, as the one director without wife or kids, mortgage or social obligations, I was the obvious volunteer.

"Besides, if you disappear," Henry had said, trying to reason with me, "look at all the alimony you'll no longer be paying Heather."

In my friends' eyes, I was the most expendable of the group. Their "logic" didn't make complete sense to me, but I was still a team player at that time, so I went along with the game plan.

Now, don't get me wrong; my oldest and truest friends didn't plan on throwing me to the wolves as the company sacrifice without *some* compensation. Henry, our CEO, owned a pretty swanky villa on Bequia and offered to let me look after it for him. Not take it over as my own residence, mind you, but he was willing to allow me to live in the boathouse on the property and manage his villa and the gardens. If I'd taken over the main house, he would have lost the substantial revenue generated through rentals to vacationers. He wanted to protect me, but he did have his limits.

The boathouse itself is more of a mini-villa overtop a boat garage, and it comes with the lap-lap of waves that lulls me to sleep at night, as well as a sizeable deck and dock combo perfect for lounging late in the afternoon, so it wasn't a bad deal for me. Throw in a new name and identity, an instant-Vincentian citizenship and passport, courtesy of a cash payout to the local government, plus a substantial contribution to my bank account promised to me by my buddies whenever the heat was off, and it didn't seem like such a bad deal at all. I could never go back to Canada—or, at least, not until people there no longer recognized me, or remembered or cared about what we had done. However, after two years on Bequia, I had yet to receive the big cash payoff, in spite of continuing promises of "soon, soon" from my not-quite-nefarious friends.

I knew that offshore banking was what had attracted Henry to Bequia in the first place as it gave him the means to avoid scrutiny from Canadian and American tax officials. In fact, I think Henry only ever visited his villa when his fingers were itchy and he felt the need to count money.

Maybe, as they claimed, the guys were still short of the ready cash they owed me. But being out of the company loop, I had to trust that what Henry told me was the truth. In any case, since the demand for petroleum geologists on Bequia was next to nil, I started up the property management business as a way of making a living until I received their compensation. In the meantime, the guys also closed their Calgary office and moved operations to Toronto. For all I knew, they just changed their venue and were on to bigger and better scams, but I was no longer privy to any of their business plans, nor did I care to be. Other than acting as Henry's property manager, I was happy to have as little as possible to do with the bunch of them.

Besides Henry's house, for which I have always charged him a handsome fee, I also manage four other villas, one of which at that time was The Clouds. I employ the Brethren, who are the two Rasta gardeners, and a couple of housekeepers, but I share a lot of the grunt work with my employees, due in part to their lack of any technical expertise and also because I have no desire to control other people. So, I too am part-time gardener and landscape designer; I look after small construction projects; often I'm the pool boy. I've even been known to wash windows, but I do draw the line at wielding a toilet brush.

Anyway, I can't complain about my current situation. I could have landed in a worse spot than this. Instead of hiding me away on Bequia, my buddies might have opted to coerce me to jump, or be tossed, out of a helicopter, like Bre-X did to Michael de Guzman.

So, here I am now, very fortunate to be living on a tropical island, running a pretty good business. I'm my own boss. I set my working hours—Monday to Saturday, 7:00 a.m. to 1:00 p.m., allowing for quality hammock time every afternoon, with Sundays and holidays off—and in this country, there are more official government holidays than work days, or so it seems. I can goof off and go fishing whenever I want, and I have great friends who like to go fishing with me. I don't pay rent or a mortgage, or even alimony any longer. And I don't have to answer to anyone.

Oh, yeah, and there's also Angie.

Angie walked onto the Sunnee Caribbee stage, and into my life, soon after I arrived on Bequia. It was her first night singing with a group of expat musicians. From the moment she opened her mouth you could hear a pin drop in the place—or maybe on the whole island, for that matter—she was so good. The voice of an angel and the looks of one, too. So, you ask, what's she doing on Bequia, if she's that good? Well, here's her story. Remember, I told you, everyone has one.

She's black, with sensuous, deep-chocolate eyes I could swim in, and braided, beaded hair that hangs to her waist. Bequia-born, her family moved to England when she was three. After having lived most of her life there, Ange considers herself British, and comes complete with a charming Brit accent, and is not at all West Indian. Her singing talent was discovered early on, then nurtured and developed by a doting mother. Angie was just as passionate about music so didn't mind the lessons, hard work, and self-promotion. She settled into a steady run of gigs as a backup singer for some of the best musicians of our time: Van Morrison, Eric Clapton, Mark Knopfler. These guys, among others, hired her not only because she's a great singer, but also because she was, and still is, drop-dead gorgeous and a class act.

The music business wore her down, though, and she couldn't keep up the pace of recording sessions and tours. She always managed to avoid the debilitating drug and booze habits of her fellow performers, but their chosen lifestyles took a toll on her, causing total disillusionment with the entire scene. Few people around her were as serious about the music business as she was. Then her mother died and Angie didn't want to stay in England without her main fan by her side. The return to Bequia was an attempt to get some rest and figure out her life. But she was preceded by her reputation. A fellow Brit, someone who'd heard her perform in England, convinced her to debut with his band of ex-pat musicians at the Sunnee Caribbee that first night we met.

Fortune smiled on me when she finished her set. As soon as I realized she was heading towards our table, I motioned Mike to move from his seat and find himself another chair, then pointed at the one he'd vacated. Angie sank down beside me.

"Hello," she said, reaching a hand out, her sultry speaking voice testifying that what I'd just heard while she performed hadn't been an act. I held that hand with a light touch and squeeze, rather than shaking it, and stared into her big brown eyes.

Melanie leaned across the table. "Angie, this is Geoff. I think he may have enjoyed your singing." Everyone laughed, but I ignored them.

And so did Angie. She spent the rest of the evening talking with me alone. After that night, she decided to remain on Bequia for good to sing several nights a week at the Sunnee Caribbee, and take up boathousekeeping with me.

As near perfect as she is, though, I do have to say Angie has one true flaw. And maybe I shouldn't even call it a flaw at all, because that sounds too negative, but she's a single-minded, independent woman who abhors having anyone tell her what to do, even if it is for her own good.

"No, I will not!" she'll say to me, often stomping around, her hands fist-clenched, while we stand in our kitchen.

What she doesn't realize is that I'm always egging her on, saying things to make her ornery, because she's even sexier when angry. Ange is one woman who knows her own mind, though, and is clear on what she wants out of life. Plus she doesn't suffer fools—or prats, pilchards, and punters, as she likes to call anyone who won't agree with that gorgeous mind of hers.

I've learned to live with this single-mindedness over the time we've been together, and I admire that liberated attitude. But her stubborn streak has managed to cause some trouble for her, and for me, from time to time, and also proved to be, in the end, what led to major problems for both of us.

This modern-woman philosophy, combined with having lived most of her life overseas where she realized public success, doesn't sit well in a traditional West Indian community, especially with chauvinistic Vincentian men. Women here may indeed raise all the children, quite often alone, and earn most of the wages, but the men of St. Vincent still manage to keep those women under their thumbs. They resent any female who doesn't need them or isn't in awe of their machismo. But in particular, they resent any black woman who co-habits with a foreign white man.

And having been born here doesn't determine acceptance by the rest of the local community, either. They think of Angie as British, a foreigner who has led a privileged life—or at least privileged in comparison to most of their lives. Because of this, she has become an anomaly and outcast among those I would have considered to be her own people. This ostracism has helped draw the two of us closer together; we're both loners and have little to do with other islanders. They consider us to be a couple of oddballs, anyway, and tend to steer clear, which is fine by me.

So, you see, in spite of being perhaps somewhat anti-social by North American standards, and even, as those very few who know, a wanted man back in Canada, I've managed to carve out a nice little niche for myself on this island and am happy with my life. Middle-aged men stuck behind office desks on any given day right across North America—or throughout Europe for all I know—fantasize about a life like this. My great luck is that I've made Everyman's dream my reality.

That is, however, until I discovered the body in the pool and my reality began turning into a nightmare.

"Geoff, hurry and get your sorry ass in here. We want to hear all the news!" Al's ex-Marine drill sergeant's voice boomed out as Angie and I walked through the gate towards the Hallidays' house. "Doc, pour that man a rum and Coke to loosen his tongue."

Our small, close-knit, group of friends had assembled to talk about recent events.

We're a motley crew and international in scope, comprised of one American, a Swiss, three Canadians—all of us Canucks holding Vincentian citizenship—an Aussie, and a Bequia-born Brit West

Indian. The Australian, laughing every time, refers to Angie as a "palmie"—his spelling. Our professions range from doctor to semi-retired sailor, artist, pilot/fisherman, singer, and property manager—so there's not much we have in common, occupation-wise. With the exception of Ange, we're all white-skinned and part of a very small collective of foreigners on this tiny island. In fact, being foreign is our one common denominator, but a genuine friendship has blossomed over the years and that's what keeps us together, keeps us meeting socially, and keeps us talking to one another.

Gossip would be what outsiders might call it, but on an island where nothing much ever happens, my friends consider these discussions over cocktails serious business. We're never malicious, unlike other wagging island-tongues, and we never set out to destroy anyone, or slander at all—unless our discussion concerns a politician. We figure politicians are fair game anywhere in the world just because they're in politics. But we will never let down the others in our immediate group by spreading rumours or doing anything less than supporting them, no matter what. We're like family. For me, they're the only real family I have.

We were eager to participate in that particular afternoon's discussion. It wasn't often any of us had first-hand information surrounding a happening. I could understand Al's impatience.

After making our greetings, Al lifted his glass and recited his usual toast: "To the best people we know."

I took that first, revitalizing sip of my drink and settled in to tell them everything, with Doc corroborating the information.

"I re-examined the body and signed the death certificate once I got back to the clinic. Geoff and I both identified her as Wilson's wife. You remember her, don't you, Al? She used to come here all the time before they were divorced."

"Yeah, I remember. And I can add that she arrived here on Saturday afternoon. I flew her from Barbados along with a guy I guessed to be her newest boyfriend. I didn't have a chance to talk to them, other than giving my safety spiel before taking off, but then Suzie and I never knew the Wilsons all that well when they were still a couple."

"Saturday was when the boyfriend told us they'd arrived. I met him at the police station when I made my report," I said. "It seems he's now Prime Suspect instead of me."

"Sarah didn't have much time on Bequia then, did she?" Melanie said, gazing off into the distance at the view from her verandah.

I knew Melanie's unwavering love for the island was behind that comment. She's what we call a Bequia-weenie—one of the legion of boosters who believes everyone else in the world is just that much less fortunate for not having been able to live here either as a permanent resident or spend lengths of time visiting the island.

"Poor woman," Melanie said, continuing. "I hope whatever happened to her was an accident, mistaken identity or something like that. It's terrible to think anyone figured they had reason to kill her."

We all remained quiet for a moment, lost in our own thoughts.

Doc broke the silence. "What else did you learn, Geoff, after you left The Clouds this morning?"

After Doc drove away from the crime scene, I locked up the house and went home to tell Angie. I knew she'd be anxious once she heard what had happened, so it was important that the news came from me first.

I pulled into the driveway and Gus ran out, greeting me with a helicopter tail-wag.

"Hey, pal," I said, patting the dog's head. "Is Ange up yet?" He looked up at me with what appeared, for a dog, to be an inquiring face, tongue hanging out the side of his mouth. Then he dashed off ahead to the closed door. I followed behind, lacking the same amount of enthusiasm, and turned the handle for both of us.

Ange was standing at the kitchen counter waiting for toast to pop. "What are you doing home? Did you forget something?"

"I wish it was because I forgot to do this before I left." I wrapped my arms around her and we kissed, long and deep.

"Well, if that were the case," she said once we broke apart, "I would hope you would surprise me like this more often. But something is wrong. What has happened?"

That's my Ange—an intuitive female to the nth degree.

"I found a dead body," I said, beginning to replay my story. She listened, without comment or expression, shaking her head when I'd finished, as though trying to rid her ears of a ringing sound. Her lips were pursed and her brow grooved.

"Oh, Geoffrey, do be careful!" she said in a mother's voice.

"Why? I didn't murder her. I have nothing to fear from the police, especially those two I met this morning."

"No, that is not what I meant. This is a small place. Whoever killed her might . . . "

"I still think I'm okay. It was probably a single act of passion, like Doc said. The murderer isn't going to be interested in me."

"Well, I am definitely not pleased that Wilson has asked you to investigate. That is a bit over the top. And I should not need to remind you of your tenuous presence on this island."

"Right," I said, gulping. "But, don't worry. I won't do anything stupid."

"Hmmm. Not so sure about that, but . . . " she said, then lightened up a bit, a tentative smile beginning to show. "Just promise you will be careful, love. You're all I have."

"Okay, since you put it that way." I looked at the stove clock. "I'd better get a move on. The Brethren will be wondering what the heck has happened. I'll come back home again after I see the police." I grazed her lips. "Oh, and Doc and Mel have invited all of us for drinks at five. Feel up to it?"

"Of course. See you later."

I left the house to check on the gardeners and then did some running around, a few business errands, trying to stretch the time before going to see the inspector to make my statement.

When I walked into the police station's reception area, two corporals and the same Sergeant Simmons from the crime scene were standing and sitting respectively, eyes glued to a TV. A commemorative plaque recognizing the donation of the television by a prominent citizen was displayed in a place of pride on the wall. People are always trying to curry favour, giving the police stuff like that—refrigerators as well—under the guise of making station life easier for the staff who have to live upstairs between shifts. But I don't think those donations are ever meant to entertain the police while they're supposed to be doing their job. These three were watching an episode of *Law and Order*. So it was possible that this was like a televised educational course and they were researching police work. When I did attract the sergeant's attention, he showed no sign of recognizing me. Without getting up from the chair he shouted at an open door, "Inspector, a white man here. Come out."

An older man walked from the adjoining office, his face appearing attentive and not at all irritated with having been summoned in such a manner by an underling. He listened while the sergeant said, "Dis de white guy who finds de body. He say he come in to makes a statement." The sergeant's gaze was pulled back to the television.

The inspector didn't seem to be vexed that his men were watching the boob tube rather than working—maybe he was more like a parent, grateful for the baby-sitting potential it offered. I would have thought a murder investigation meant extra hours and overtime pay for everyone, but then perhaps this inspector just practiced different management methods than I did. Or maybe he was so close to retirement he didn't care any longer.

"Yes, thank you for coming," he said. "Inspector Kydd."

As though afraid of touching, he sort of air-shook my offered hand with his own when he turned to me. "I want you to meet someone, then I will ask both of you to accompany me to my office. I will take your statement, as well, if you do not mind." His voice lacked the usual dialect I'd become accustomed to hearing the other local police speak, suggesting that this inspector may have received his education at the more posh Boys' Grammar School over on St. Vincent. And his manner matched his precise pronunciation and was just as stiff and formal as a dress uniform.

I offered a slight nod in agreement.

Turning to the sergeant, he said, "Bring out de prisoner."

Simmons dragged his eyes away from the television, glanced over at me, and sighed. He stood up in no great hurry, as though in pain, and ambled through a doorway at the back of the room. There was nothing wrong with him, though. He was just in no rush for anyone's sake, and especially not mine.

While we waited, the inspector said, "I am sure de case will close now in short order. We found de murderer."

I looked at him and wondered if he should be telling me anything—giving information to someone who also might be a suspect in the case. I didn't reply at all, though, as Kydd's attention had already drifted over to the television screen. Shaking my head in disbelief, I turned away to look out the open front door, into the roadway. A nanny goat, in the company of twin kids, had been tied to a stake to graze on the scrubby patch of lawn next to the cement path.

The sergeant soon returned with a tall man, built like an athlete, who looked to be in his early thirties. He was dressed in a polo shirt, khaki shorts, and sandals—all recognizable and expensive brand-name clothing. Stretching out a hand, he introduced himself.

"Hi, I'm Ned Watson," he said, amiable, like he was at a cocktail party. Then he added, "I'm Sarah's boyfriend . . . Was her boyfriend. I came with her on this trip because she asked me to. I didn't kill her though. I never would have killed her."

Definitely an American, I thought—open and ready to tell you his life story at the drop of a hat, like so many other Yanks I've met.

"Mr. Watson is de dead woman's boyfriend, like he say." Inspector Kydd said with self-satisfaction. "He came to de station this morning and reported her missing, but he tells me he has not actually seen her since they had dinner together last night. I decided to hold Mr. Watson for further questioning and will send him over to police headquarters in St. Vincent this afternoon to be charged. I am waiting for orders from de commissioner."

Reserved as he had been earlier, the inspector was experiencing some difficulty holding back his excitement at the thought of having solved the crime in such short order and without help.

Watson turned to me. His initial casual demeanour now shaken, his eyes wide with panic. "I didn't do it! I've been telling them, over and over, since I came in that I didn't do it. Please, you have to believe me. No one here will listen. I would never have harmed Sarah. I don't know who did, but it wasn't me. Please help me," he said, his hands stretched out. "I came here to report she was missing. Would I have done that if I'd been the one who killed her?"

Watson was big, strong and, I thought, capable of physical violence if driven to it. But I studied him for a few moments and saw genuine fear in his eyes. He was telling the truth. Besides, I wasn't sure if, given the opportunity, he would know which end of a gun he should point.

"Could we all sit down somewhere and get a few things sorted out, Inspector?" I said. "Maybe Mr. Watson," I waved a hand in Ned's direction, "can give us information to help solve this. Then you'll be able to write up your report."

Kydd looked at me, blinking a couple of times, while he mulled the idea over. Then he said, "Well, all right. De two of you come into my office."

Pointing at the door from which he'd appeared earlier, Kydd entered the room ahead of us, as though taking it for granted we would follow and not make a sudden bolt for freedom. I closed the door behind me, shutting out the din of the TV, which was now showing an old episode of *The Cosby Show*. So, it was true after all— the television had been installed in the station for the purpose of entertaining the office staff.

Besides the inspector's chair, one other was positioned on the opposite side of the desk. Kydd turned to a corner of the room and removed a pile of files, papers, and assorted junk, unearthing a folding chair. Once that was cleaned off, Ned picked it up and moved it next to where I was already seated. He sat down. The inspector had already settled in at the other side of the desk. Taking a pad of foolscap paper and a pen out of a drawer, he wrote the date at the top of the page.

He turned to me first, and said, "State your full name, please."

It dawned on me that he was writing up the crime report. On a pad of paper. In long hand. And his penmanship was beautiful. I glanced around the office. No sign of a computer, not even an old typewriter, just a couple of filing cabinets, drawers open and full to overflowing. Paper was stacked everywhere on other surfaces around the room, like a tiny hurricane had hit the place at one time. I hadn't remembered noticing either a computer or a typewriter in the reception area out front, either. No wonder the police on Bequia had difficulty doing their jobs. The single piece of equipment they'd been issued was a television set.

Once I had given Kydd all my particulars and told him every-thing I knew, it was Watson's turn.

"Sarah and I met in the States. I was her personal trainer." A fact accounting for his perfect build. And hers, too, come to think of it. "We got along so well, we started dating after a couple of training sessions. Sarah was one good-looking woman."

I could understand the attraction. In spite of their obvious age difference, which I pegged to be almost twenty years, the two of them must have been a hot couple.

Hesitating a moment, he cleared his throat, where a protrud-ing Adam's apple was bobbing up and down. His face was pale, in spite of the salon-tan colouring. "The trip to Bequia was Sarah's idea. All I can tell you about her reason for coming was she said she needed to get some information, firsthand, possibly something to do with her ex. I never knew exactly. She didn't offer any details. But I got the impression she hoped to find out something she could use to blackmail Mr. Wilson. I really don't know." He stopped to think some more, sucking on his lower lip. Then he added, "I do know there was some kind of large settlement between the Wilsons when they separated, but Sarah told me she'd recently experienced finan-cial setbacks—a failed business or something."

Maybe Sarah had been going back to the well for another dip of the bucket and was looking for information to use against Wil-son, I thought.

Watson finished, saying, "She never told me anything about her background or personal finances, so I'm speculating here."

"No more speculating, please, Mr. Watson," Kydd said. "Leave that to me and my men. Tell me what happened after you arrived on Bequia, up until de time you last saw de woman."

"After we arrived at the airport Saturday evening, I was with Sarah all the time, until Sunday night," Ned said, turning to look at me. "I didn't see her speaking with anyone, except to greet old acquaintances, but never what you would call a real conversation. There was one guy who signalled her away from our table. That was on Sunday evening at the restaurant. She got up and followed him outside so I couldn't hear what they talked about, but she came back fast afterwards, almost at a run, and alone. She looked worried, and her eyes and nose were red, like she'd been crying, but she wouldn't tell me anything."

He stopped speaking when Kydd held up a hand. The inspector wrote at the speed of light in order to catch up, then said, "Continue."

"I thought Sarah seemed changed after that." Ned looked back at me again. "If I had to describe it, she looked old all of a sudden, like she did the one time I saw her without makeup, as though the wind had been knocked out of her. She had always been serious during this trip, but after that conversation she was quiet—too quiet. That concerned me, and I told her so, but she still wouldn't talk to me about it. We went back to the hotel room after dinner and, I can't say for sure, but I think she took a phone call while I was in the shower. I know I heard the phone ring. When I came out from the bathroom, she said she was meeting a friend and didn't expect to be back right away. She told me not to wait up. That was the last time I saw her."

Watson's eyes teared up as he finished speaking, and he wiped across both eyes with a rough finger. The inspector continued writing without noticing. I looked around the room but didn't see a box of tissues. Ned Watson was nothing but a gentle giant, more brawn than brain. He'd convinced me, there and then, that he couldn't have been the one who murdered Sarah.

"I'm sorry for your loss," I said, mumbling the condolences, while averting my eyes up to the corner of the ceiling, allowing him some privacy.

After finishing what he was writing, Kydd looked across the table at Watson. He dug into a pocket of his pants to pull out a rumpled handkerchief that had seen better days and offered it. Watson was already using a forearm to finish the job.

When his composure was regained, and the inspector's hankie re-pocketed, I said, "Would you recognize the guy who spoke with Sarah in the restaurant?"

Great! It seemed that now I was conducting the questioning as well as the investigation.

Kydd didn't try to stop me, but instead, leaning towards Watson with curiosity, he set his pen down and laid his hands flat on the table.

"I think so," Ned said. "There were a lot of people around. It seemed like a pretty popular spot, but I feel sure I would know him again. He was African-American, short, youngish."

Well, great! That description certainly narrowed things down somewhat. Out of an indigenous population of fifty-five hundred, about ninety-five percent are black and young, and fifty percent of them are male.

"Can you be more specific?" I said. "Do you have any other information we can go on?"

Ned shook his head. "He was too far away for me to see anything else."

Turning away from him, I glanced at Kydd and said, "Maybe before you ship him over to St. Vincent, Inspector, you might want to think about driving Mr. Watson around the island to see if he can find and identify this guy he's talking about. If you do find him, it's possible you could uncover more information about what Sarah did after leaving the hotel room."

"You might have a point," he said, nodding his head in thoughtful agreement. "I'll get de car and drive it myself. We'll begin at de restaurant."

Now the guy was thinking. I stopped short of saying it was better not to solve the crime at all than hang the wrong man. I wasn't too sure what the advice limit was on how the police should do their job, considering it hadn't been all that long a time since I was Prime Suspect myself.

We all stood up to leave, but before Ned or I could open the door, Kydd called us back. "One moment, gentlemen. I wonder if you could find it in your hearts to make a small donation. We are building a new Methodist church on Bequia and I am sure God would smile on you both if you make, say, a twenty-dollar donation. Each." His jaw was set in a stern manner. He glared first at me then at Ned, square into our eyes,

I couldn't help thinking that the investigation would grind to a complete halt unless its wheels were greased. Ned and I looked at each other. He shrugged and pulled out his wallet. I did the same, but cursed to myself because I always seem to get caught by these people seeking financial assistance for one cause or another. That was the first time a policeman had ever tapped into me, though, other than to sell me tickets to the annual Policeman's Ball. Typical. Everyone has their hand out to take advantage of whatever situation comes their way—even murder, it seems. I made a mental note to add the donation to Wilson's expense account.

"You know," Mike said, "I was drinking at Bob's last night. I saw Sarah and—what did you say his name was? Ned?" He paused and whistled. "Too right I remember her. She's a looker! She always turned heads on the beach when she was still married to Wilson. But I didn't know her well enough to say g'day last night." Being Australian, and plugged into many of Bequia's social drinking groups, it didn't surprise any of us that he just happened to be in Bob's Bar at the same time.

Mike is a part-time resident who moors *O Lucky Me!* in the Harbour. He struck it rich in the Australian lottery a few years back and now spends about six months at a time on Bequia, sailing here every Easter (the end of Australian summer) in his live-aboard, home-built dream boat, leaving behind a wife and a couple of kids. Mike and his wife have a flexible marriage agreement; she doesn't like to sail, preferring to stay at home, but doesn't mind Mike taking off for half a year at a time. Maybe she's happy to be rid of him for six months, as he claims is the case. She has nothing to worry about anyway, as he always returns at the end of his extended visits to Bequia. We know of other couples carrying on long-distance marriages like Mike's, so to us it's not an unusual arrangement. At least he does leave her well looked after. He's also loyal without a fault, as his only other loves in life are his boat and beer.

Mike enjoys the locally brewed beer, Hairoun, in particular, and takes every opportunity to quaff large quantities whenever he's in residence. Yet he never gets drunk; he's just very sociable. In fact, Mike is such a likable guy that every clique wants to include him. Ours is one of many expatriate groups that invites Mike whenever we get together, happy to number him among our good friends. He manages to fit in well. With all his various connections, he's also privy to every little thing that's happening on the island at any given time, so we look to him as a constant source of news and local opinion.

"Unfortunately," Mike said, "I don't have any more information about the Wilsons. But, now you've told your story I'll keep my ears and eyes open, Geoff, and let you know of any gossip I glean."

"Thanks, mate," I said. "Anyone else know anything?" They all gave it some thought, but in the end shook their heads in a collective no. While the Hallidays and Al and Suzie have lived on Bequia years longer than Mike, Angie, or me, none ever had dealings with either of the Wilsons, and what they knew of the couple's past history was through the never-ending island gossip.

I'm making this sound as though we're just a bunch of old biddies with nothing better to do than talk about other people and revel in their misfortune. But like I said, our gossip is never intended to be malicious. We have a great group of friends, all good people. Our ages run from early thirties to mid fifties, but despite that disparity there are a number of things that keep us together and enjoying each other's company. For one thing, we all love to eat good food, and Melanie's dinner parties are legendary, always a great source of entertainment. For me, it's been an easy camaraderie with the rest of them, a friendship involving not only a healthy amount of playful joking, but also solid support for one another whenever it's needed.

Other than Mike, no one in the group has any children or strong family ties back home in our respective countries of origin. My friends are also not judgemental, nor have they been even the least bit curious about my past—of which I've told them nothing, by the way, not even my real name. They bought my invented story hook, line, and sinker, never questioning me further. So, in a way, we've become family for one another, celebrating birthdays and holidays, mucking in together. They're a good bunch of people, these friends of mine, and Angie and I have felt privileged knowing them. I'm one fortunate guy!

And enjoying a sundowner with these friends is something of a ritual. By the time I'd finished talking, it was getting on to six-thirty. The Hallidays have a great view of the western sky from their place; in fact, their verandah has a sweeping panorama of the entirety of Admiralty Bay, from the headland at Hamilton, where my boathouse is situated, around to the centre of Port Elizabeth, and right on down to the southern tip of the island at West Cay. The Halliday house, or *Nice Scene* as the locals have named it, is a perfect place to enjoy a drink as well as the evening spectacle. And the conditions were excellent that late afternoon, with not a single wisp of cloud in the sky or, in particular, on the horizon, to obstruct the setting sun.

We remained solemn while waiting as the now-orange orb melted into the water. Then we raised our glasses to the much anticipated, and brilliant, green flash, an atmospheric phenomenon visible to the naked eye only under perfect conditions. You can google it for more of an explanation and some great pictures—although nothing online is as spectacular as witnessing it in person. We were rewarded that afternoon when it seemed to last for an entire second. After the show was over, and as the darkness of the evening set in, we all scattered our separate ways. The Hallidays were staying home that night; Angie had to sing; Al and Suzie promised to meet Angie and me later, after dinner.

As we were leaving the Hallidays' house, Mike pulled me off to one side.

"Are you interested in doing a little investigating tonight? We could start off at Bob's, try to pick up on any gossip circulating around Lower Bay, then meet the others at the Sunnee Caribbee."

"I'm game. What about Al? Shouldn't we ask him to join us?"

"No, it might make for too many. We're further ahead with only the two of us. Don't want to be conspicuous. Al kind of has a way of attracting attention. Besides, I doubt Suzie would let him go."

"Too true," I said, laughing. Al's kept on a short tether.

"My dinghy is beached down there, anyway, so I need to hitch a ride."

"Okay, you're on. Angie can drive us to the bar then she'll still have time to go home and get ready for her gig. Let me confirm again with Al and Suzie that they'll meet us later at the hotel. And Mike," I said, grabbing hold of his arm, "I appreciate your help with this."

"Hell! What are mates for?"

We strolled into Bob's Beach Bar about fifteen minutes later; it wasn't quite a hopping place, but then the evening was still young. I had never made a habit of drinking in that particular bar. A little rough around the edges and too much local colour for my taste, it just didn't appeal to me. My friends and I tend to patronize the more touristy establishments in the Harbour, those providing live music. The sole entertainment supplied by Bob's is drinking, and lots of it. I've been told the restaurant serves solid local cuisine, albeit leaning towards various combinations of heavy, starchy foods and chicken. But never having eaten there, I can't comment on the quality.

Mike went up to the bar and ordered beer while I chose a table. He joined me, setting down three bottles—two for him, one for me. Always one for a dramatic entrance, he swung a leg over the back of his chair and sat down. I eased onto my chair normally. We both scrutinized the other clientele: some looked as though they'd been in those same seats since the previous night, and maybe that was true. Mike stood up again and walked over to speak with a couple of guys at a table by the door. When he returned he had nothing new to report.

"They say they were here last night, too. I didn't see them my-self, but I know they're regulars. Thought they'd probably made an appearance at some time during the evening. They told me nothing happened while they were here, but they did hear, already, about the murder."

"That figures. Everybody and his dog must know by now. What about the bartender?"

"Nah, different guy," Mike said, glancing at the bar. "The own-er was working the bar last night. I don't see him anywhere now. I don't know this bartender." He waggled a thumb in the direction of the local boy leaning on the other side of the counter, a bored expression on his face. Mike looked back at me. "He's new. Doesn't look old enough to be allowed to pour alcohol let alone drink it, does he?"

"Hey, maybe I should look for the owner, see if he knows any-thing about Sarah."

"It wouldn't hurt to ask," Mike said, taking another swig of beer.

But I wasn't all that anxious to seek out Hermut Landecker or start investigating on my own, so I remained seated, ripping at the beer label.

We talked to each other in hushed voices awhile longer, not wanting to be overheard. A few more people drifted in and out of the bar past our table. For the most part, they looked to be Lower Bay locals; some came in for a quick stand at the bar either to down a shot of rum or buy a beer to walk with, as they say; others joined people already sitting at tables. Even though the place was begin-ning to fill up, nothing else was happening and no one came in who looked to have even a remote connection with the Wilsons. Our in-vestigation seemed dead in the water before it had begun. We knew we wouldn't get any help from these patrons. I'd never seen such a sorry bunch of hard-luck cases.

One guy walked in and sat at the bar by himself. After being served, he exchanged a few words with the bartender. I recognized him. A big bruiser, he also had the ugliest face I've ever seen, a fea-ture that had led to his being nicknamed Pigface by fellow locals. His nose looked as though it hadn't been set by a competent orthopaedic surgeon the last time it was broken, and his face and neck were scattered with pockmarks, either from a bad case of acne or the result of some sadist denting him all over with a large blunt instrument. Everyone on Bequia seems to have an alias anyway, but this one suited more than most. Although I think if anyone ever had the nerve to use it directly to his face they might not live long enough to draw another breath.

Pigface must have sensed I was staring at him. He turned around to look at me then flashed a big, gold-toothed smile my way. I nodded, embarrassed to be caught staring, and shuddered to myself as soon as he turned back to the bar, away from me.

"Let's get out of here. This place gives me the creeps," I said in a whisper to Mike. "Besides, I don't think we're going to get any information out of this lot tonight."

"Okay," he said, downing the remaining beer from the second bottle. "We can take my dinghy over to the Sunnee Caribbee. I left it tied to a tree earlier. Maybe we should pick up a roti" (curry in a wrap), "at the Boley. I'm half-starved. Mel's appetizers were great, but I could use more protein swirling around in my stomach to mix with all this beer."

As we walked along the road not far from the bar, we passed a group of people lounging around on the grassy area between the road and the beach. They'd pulled a few old broken-down couches and chairs, even a set of conjoined airplane seats, into a circle and had managed to design a makeshift living room under the stars. Rap music blared from an enormous boom box at a tiny bar/shack called The Rasta Ranch. Most of the people gathered around were sitting, comatose, listening to—or being accosted by—the loud music that didn't allow for much coherent, let alone intelligent, conversation. A couple of rough-looking guys were starting to exchange heated words and were shoving each other, a situation we knew could deteriorate with lightning speed into an all-out fight, so Mike and I picked up our own pace.

Under his breath, Mike said, "Looks as though there must have been a crack delivery recently."

"It ruins Bequia, doesn't it? What must the tourists think?"

"Too right. Best to avoid it and turn a blind eye whenever you can—that's my philosophy."

Crack cocaine has become available throughout the country and has been in heavy use in recent years on Bequia. We can all tell when a shipment hits the island, even though we're not in the least connected with it. Robberies increase as addicts attempt to raise cash by whatever means possible to pay for their habits. This advent of crack has created a dirty underside to an otherwise pretty nice little island. Lower Bay in particular has always been a bad place for the stuff—another reason I don't like to go there to drink. It's a shame, too, because the beach itself at Lower Bay is one of the best on the island, and a great place to swim.

Once we'd launched Mike's dinghy from the beach, it took a few minutes to motor out past Princess Margaret Beach and tie up at the Sunnee Caribbee dock. The bright hotel-bar lights were a welcome contrast and relief after the dim lighting and seedy patrons we'd left behind at Bob's. Mike insisted on going to the Green Boley first, a short distance down the walkway, to pick up something to eat. It was still early, anyway. By the time we finished our chicken rotis and walked back to the Sunnee Caribbee, Al and Suzie were already sitting at a table. We ordered drinks from the waiter. Angie was about to begin singing her first set, so we settled in to enjoy.

About twenty minutes later, Angie joined us while the musicians performed a few instrumental numbers. The others chatted, but my attention wandered as I surveyed the bar and patio area. The place was pretty full for a Monday night in July. A Windjammer cruise, the *Mandalay*, had arrived in the Harbour that day and most of the bar patrons were passengers on shore for an evening of entertainment and fruity alcoholic beverages. They all wore vacation-requisite parrot-coloured party shirts and dresses that shouted to the rest of the world, "We're in a tropical paradise and having a great time. Wish you were here!"

Then I noticed Pigface sitting at the bar on the other side of the patio opposite to us, talking with the bartender. The better lighting confirmed the fact—he was one ugly guy.

I wasn't surprised to see him there after he'd just been at Bob's. It's usual for local men to make the rounds of bars every evening searching for tourists who, they hope, might look after their financial needs. Many prey on single, white, foreign women who are themselves just out for a fun night of *wining*, an erotic-in-the-extreme form of coupling that passes for dancing here—what Al calls "sex standing up." Some of these unsuspecting women end up becoming sugar mamas or, worse, punching bags. In the case of Pigface, any prospective woman he had hopes of cruising would have to be blind as well as rich.

Pigface swivelled on his chair and caught my eye. Before I could turn away, he leaned back against the bar, pointed a finger, cocked it like a gun, and mimicked that he was shooting me, laughing the whole time. I spun around and gulped, but didn't let on to anyone at the table what had just happened. I downed my entire drink in one chug and, without hesitation, signalled the waiter over and ordered two more.

Once Angie had finished singing for the night and the passengers were loaded onto the last tender heading back to their cruise ship, the place pretty well cleared out in no time. There were a few local men left, either propping up posts, beer bottle in hand, or dancing, by themselves, swaying less than a foot in front of too-large speakers, the deafening sound as well as alcohol making them totally oblivious to their surroundings. Pigface had vanished.

I'd had a few too many drinks myself by that point and was feeling an alcoholic-happy glow throughout my body, the earlier problems of my day somewhat forgotten.

Angie said goodnight to the band. Mike left us and set off down to the end of the dock, where he'd tied his dinghy. Angie and I walked with Al and Suzie to the hotel parking lot and the taxi that was waiting. Al and I shook hands goodbye while the women air-kissed. Al and Susie climbed in. As they drove away, Al said, shouting, "Remember your promise!"

"What promise? What was that all about?" I asked, mumbling to Angie after we got into our own car. She was the designated driver. I looked over at her beautiful face.

"Don't worry. You'll find out soon enough."

I met her glance then we both turned to look as the dashboard clock clicked over to midnight. I dragged my eyes back to look at Ange again.

She smiled and said, "Very soon, as a matter of fact."

I couldn't remember the rest of the drive home—or even crawling into bed, for that matter, let alone any promises I'd made. I must have had more to drink than I'd realized, but it had been much more than a typical stressful day, after all. That evening out with my friends had been necessary to allow me to unwind as well as to forget.

Chapter Three

"Hey, Geoff-ie boy! It's four a.m. and the fish are biting!"

I could have sworn Al was standing right over me, shouting in my face, but when I opened my eyes I realized he was outside, calling from way down at the end of our dock.

He'd wakened me from a dead sleep. I rolled over on my back and groaned, then mumbling, said, "Please tell me I'm dreaming, Ange."

"Well, it's your own fault for mentioning fishing while he was drinking last night." Angie's voice conveyed not the least shred of sympathy. "There's some cheese and bread in the fridge. You'd better pack something. You know the only thing Al will have brought for the trip is beer. Have fun."

Angie turned away from me and feigned sleep. Our trusty hound, the usual alarm clock, hadn't even twitched during all of this, and was snuggling even closer to my girl. Right where I should have been. The lucky dog!

Going fishing at such an ungodly hour must have been the promise I'd made to Al the previous night. Knowing this trip was inevitable, because if I didn't go I'd never hear the end of it, I rolled off the bed, pulled on a pair of shorts and a T-shirt, and went out onto the small adjoining verandah. Waving, I said, "I'll be right down," and descended the stairs from our bedroom loft to the kitchen. As well as cheese and bread, I found a few small mangoes and tossed everything into a bag. Grabbing a tube of sunblock from the bathroom, I put on a hat, pocketed my sunglasses, slipped into a pair of flip-flops, and made my way to the end of the dock where Al's fishing boat, the *Suzie-Q*, a 1971 Hattras 44', was idling. The sky was still pitch-black dark.

"Don't you ever sleep?" I said as I walked up to Al.

"Not when there's a chance to go fishing. Hop in, man. I have a feeling we're going to catch a big one today."

No one should feel that chipper at four in the morning, particularly if they've been drinking with me the night before and I'm hung over.

I climbed into the boat and settled myself while Al put the engines in reverse, backed away from the boathouse dock, turned the boat, and motored out of the Harbour. We were soon heading due west, the next closest landfall in that direction being Central America, about eighteen hundred miles away.

"Why didn't you invite Mike?" Why is it that I'm Al's only friend who's always made to suffer? Life just doesn't seem fair some days.

"You actually invited him yourself. In fact, I think you invited everyone in the bar, at one point, but Mike said he couldn't make it today. It's Tuesday. Remember? Ladies' Luncheon at Mac's."

Oh, right. I'd forgotten Mike's hectic social schedule. Everyone loves his company so he gets invited to everything, including a once-a-week lunch with the biggest group of gossips on the island. They'd made him an honorary lady, the sole man ever to be accepted as an equal because he's the one person they can count on to have more news about local events than they ever hear. I was sure Sarah's murder would be the main entrée on their menu.

Deciding to make the most of the ride, I closed my eyes and was beginning to fall back to sleep when Al said, "Did I ever tell you how lucky I am?"

Well, only about ten thousand times, I thought, knowing I was in for hearing the full story yet one more time, whether I wanted to or not. Al was on to his favourite subject—Suzie. I had long ago discovered my best defence in this conversation with Al, which is just a monologue and not a conversation at all, is to nod at appropriate places and maintain a long-distance gaze. I proceeded to do so.

"I don't know what that little Swiss Miss sees in me, but I'm forever grateful there's something in here that makes her want to stay." Grinning like an idiot, he tapped his chest in pride.

Rolling my eyes, I then closed them and kept them that way. Bad enough I had to listen to his bragging; I didn't need to witness the self-satisfied gestures as well.

The exact reason why Suzie sticks with him has often eluded the rest of us, too. Al can be rough and crude at times, but he has an honest heart, and he's been my truest friend on Bequia ever since I arrived. He's the kind of pal who would not just give you the shirt off his back, but also his shoes and socks as well—that is, if he wore them. And he'd never do anything expecting the same in return. As far as he's concerned, that's what good friends do—be there for each other, no questions asked. And, knowing Al as I do, it's far better to have him as a friend than an enemy.

To say Al has lived a varied life is an understatement. He's American-born and, as he himself admits, comes from a long line of dirt-poor Southerners—trailer-park trash. He's of medium build and has a full beard and a swarthy, windblown look about him—the perfect appearance for a sea captain.

Al joined the Marines as soon as he was of age, and that early training and discipline has stood him well throughout his life. Yet he still maintains an easy casualness, due to an innate Southern gentlemanliness. He tends to fit in well with most people he meets, once they get to know him. Al can be a pretty likeable guy. However, like Ange, he doesn't suffer fools and is not afraid to speak up about what's on his mind, so the politically correct segment of society has never been too impressed by his forthrightness. But then, he's never been overly enamoured by the politically correct, either.

He had planned on being career military. Then the Gulf War came along. Al served with distinction as a fighter helicopter pilot but was injured during the campaign and discharged on a disability pension soon after the war ended. He's always walked with a slight limp since, although his injury wasn't bad enough to slow him at all.

Rather than return to the States and settle down, Al began a "grand tour of Europe," as he likes to call it, to have a look at the world and see what was out there. Well, he made it solo as far as a ferry ride to Crete, where Suzette, a Swiss artist, tripped him up.

Not surprising, though, as she's gorgeous, a petite blonde with the most calm, even-tempered, sunny disposition known to mankind. With not a single mean bone in her body, she's the total opposite to Al in many ways, and they do say that opposites attract.

There must have been magic in the air over that ferry boat the day they met, because they've been together for the past ten years and are still head-over-heels in love with each other. We all believe that, had it not been for Suzette, Al would have done himself some serious damage by now. Suzie keeps him on an even keel.

They bought a sailboat soon after meeting and didn't take long to make their way from the Mediterranean to the Caribbean. Weighing anchor in Admiralty Bay about seven years ago, and bitten by the Bequia bug, they sold their sailboat, built a house, and have lived here ever since.

Al saw the opportunity to use his piloting skills and started up a private charter company when the Bequia airport was built. He's done well enough with his business to allow them a comfortable life. Suzie continues with her painting, and he indulges himself with "big toys for big boys," as he calls them, like his airplane and fishing boat.

So, Al's three passions—Suzie, flying, and fishing—are the major focuses of his daily life. And he loves to tell everyone about his great fortune every chance he gets. He does have a tendency to bore those of us who have heard it all before, but there's something endearing about a crusty salt whose own wife still excites him.

Al also enjoys reliving his military past with a covert subscription to *Soldier of Fortune Magazine*—a small quirk in his otherwise peaceful and happy existence.

"Geoff, why don't you grab us a couple of brews out of the fridge? Actually, make mine one of those fine ciders Angie brought back from England." Al's request came in the middle of another of my attempts to catch some much-needed shut-eye.

Under normal circumstances I would have considered it a little early for beer *or* cider, but I was getting thirsty. I knew there'd be nothing else on board to drink, except maybe water, so I resigned myself to quenching my thirst with Al's preference, thinking that alcoholic fruit would constitute a better breakfast drink than hops. I went into the galley.

Yanking open the small bar fridge door, I was surprised to see nothing. "Sorry, Al, it looks like you drank everything. The fridge, she is empty."

"That can't be," he said, as I ducked out of the galley. He looked puzzled. "I asked Boney to fill it up yesterday on the chance I could talk you into joining me this morning. He's never let me down before."

Boney is Al's sole crewmember and he looks after the fishing boat. In exchange, Al lets him sleep on it.

"And it sounds like the fridge wasn't the only thing Boney forgot to fill." Al pointed downwards, the other hand cupped behind his ear. "Listen! The right engine is about to die . . ." He raised his finger as I realized the constant humming from below had diminished by half. Then, as Al pointed to the left of the deck, the other engine cut out soon after as it too ran dry.

"Damn! I should have checked the gas before we left." Al slapped the wheel. "Boney's always been so reliable. I'm accustomed to depending on him to have everything done and the boat ready whenever I want to use it." Al shook his head, more in disappointment than anger.

I looked off the stern at the horizon from where we had come and then all around. Nothing. No sight of land anywhere. But worse than not being able to see land was knowing no one on land could see us—nor would they have any idea where we were, for that matter.

"I'll get on the radio, see if we can find someone who has cold beer and also wants to rescue us." Al was still in good humour, in spite of the situation. He swung himself into the galley, but his voice echoed up to me a few seconds later. "I'm afraid I have more bad news, man. It looks as though we didn't run out of gas through Boney's negligence. The radio is toast." Al's head poked out through the galley entrance. "The set's busted. We've been sabotaged."

We stared at each other. All of a sudden, I was wide, wide awake.

Then Al brightened up again. "I guess I'll finally be able to use my emergency flares for something other than a substitute for New Year's Eve fireworks in the Harbour. Let's hope they still work." He turned back and disappeared into the galley. I could hear him rummaging below. Now that the engines were silent, we could have heard one of their shear pins go.

This time when Al emerged on deck, box of flares in hand, he stopped dead and stared towards the east. The rising sun was making the morning look as though it was the beginning of another clear and brilliant day.

"Hel-lo," Al said, murmuring. "I think company's coming."

I followed Al's gaze, then squinted, but couldn't see a thing. "Where? Are you sure?"

Quite matter-of-factly, Al said, "I can see over the horizon. Go get the binoculars."

I threw him a disbelieving glance, but did as he asked. We've been friends so long I know I should never question any of his claims, no matter how far-fetched they sound.

Back on deck, I scanned the horizon with the binoculars, following Al's pointing finger, and eventually picked up the faintest speck, growing larger by the second, just as the distant whine of a boat's engine hit my ears.

"They're gaining on us, fast," Al said. "It must be a cigarette boat." They're the high-speed boats preferred for running drugs up and down the coast, because they always outperform anything used by the coast guard. "They'll be here in no time. Keep an eye on it." Al spun around and went to work.

He opened doors and hatches and a few other hidey-holes that would have been known only to him. While I watched the other boat advance, behind my back I heard the metallic clicks of Al assembling something. Through the binoculars, the boat was coming closer.

"Ta da!" Al said, announcing that he'd finished. "Haven't had this together for a while. Hope she still works."

I pivoted to see Al holding a shotgun.

"My baby," he said, caressing it. "A twelve-gauge Remington Marine Stainless Steel Pump."

"Uh, what if they saw us stalled, couldn't raise us on the VHF, and are actually coming to rescue us?"

"Well, as the Boy Scouts always say, 'Be Prepared,'" he said, smiling.

I wanted to feel reassured; I'd never in my life been in a situation that required the use of guns. I didn't say a word, just licked my parched lips. I could have used a cold beer to drench them and my equally dry mouth.

"I may not have to use this thing, but I doubt we were sabotaged only so some guys in a cigarette boat could play good citizens and rescue us. You'd better get below deck, Geoff. This could get ugly, and the last thing I need is you fainting or, worse, puking and creating a mess of my boat."

The blood drained from my face, making me lightheaded, but I did as Al said, knowing I'd be a total, useless screw-up, anyway. Hiding in the galley, I made sure I had a clear view of the boat's stern.

I gripped the flare with a sweaty hand, hoping I could follow Al's directions, if the time came to use it, and that my drenching sweat wouldn't render the thing useless.

The other boat was close enough now that I was able to count three people on board. We were outnumbered and I didn't have a weapon, or the stomach to use one even if I did. I'm not a religious man, but I decided praying was a good idea and sent heavenward an entreaty that Al knew what he was doing, just in case he required divine intervention. He hid on deck as the other boat pulled alongside the *Suzie-Q*.

Two of the guys, one with a pistol, the other brandishing a cutlass, were preparing to board—Pistol-guy was ready to grab our gunwale and Cutlass-guy picked up a painter to tie on—while the third one killed the engine. Then I heard Al's voice as he greeted them.

"Hi, sailors, new in town?"

Blam! Blam! Blam! followed in quick succession.

A moment later, Al said, "It's okay, Geoff, you can come out now."

I did, my heart adding substance to the cotton ball already stuck in my mouth.

"You see, the thing is, these boys think they're all hot shit because they can drive a fast boat loaded with drugs and outrun the coast guard, but they really do make piss-poor pirates." Al took a deep breath, expelling air like a slow hiss from a pressure hose. He was somewhat cool and composed, but the gun shook in his grip and one eye twitched, something I had never seen before.

He regained self-control without missing a beat. "Right. Let's clean up this mess and get back home to the women." He set down the shotgun.

One of the bodies, the driver's, had fallen into the cigarette boat. The other two were sprawled over *Suzie-Q*'s gunwale. We tossed both bodies back into the other boat and followed them in, once Al had secured the painter. When we flipped the bodies over, I recognized Pigface.

"I saw this guy last night. He must have been following me," I said, whispering. "Who are the others?"

"Why are you whispering?" Al said, booming again. "They're dead. They can't hear you. I recognize them though. The other two are from St. Vincent, but they're equally bad shit like Pigface. I've heard they were all heavily involved in the drug trade. I don't know why the police have never picked them up. Seems like a no-brainer to me, since everyone knows their rep. The only place any of them should have been for years is locked up behind bars."

Their occupation would have been moving shipments of cocaine and crack along this country's coastline, a segment of the illegal substances' northbound journey from Columbia and Venezuela to the States. Why they had been after us might now remain a mystery.

After a look around their boat, Al said, "Good, their radio's working. When we've cleaned up the mess over here, I'll radio back to Bequia and let everyone know we hooked into something big. The story is we found this boat and its dead passengers drifting, just as they are now, okay? I wouldn't want word to get around about my disassembled popgun, especially as it's slightly illegal. Boney doesn't even know it exists, and I'd like Suzette to think that playing with firearms and weapons is a distant memory for me. Let's just say the Swiss Miss is too nice to be mixing with guns. I prefer to keep those two parts of my life separate."

I knew Al divided his life into eras: Before Suzette and After Suzette.

"Al, when you said your gun is only slightly illegal, what did you mean?"

"Well, it's not registered, but I rarely put it together as an actual weapon, so it's really only illegal when in use. But I doubt anyone would ever have the smarts to assemble it, even if they did manage to find all the parts. That's my assurance that it's not the least bit dangerous."

"Oh," was all I could answer. I wasn't sure the authorities would accept his reasoning, but it seemed to make sense to me.

We dipped buckets in the sea, washed all the blood off Al's boat, and tossed the empty shotgun shells over the side. Then Al disassembled his gun, cleaning and fondling each piece before stowing it back in its individual hiding place. When he was satisfied with the state of his own boat, he boarded the other.

"We'll siphon some of their gas over to my engines and go home under our own steam. That way no one will know we actually ran out."

With the transfer complete, Al radioed Bequia to alert the police. He was about to reboard *Suzie-Q* when he spotted a cooler.

"Oh, look. How thoughtful. They brought along some cold drinks." Inside were about twenty bottles of Hairoun and a six-pack of cider. "My cider! Well, now there's no doubt. We were set up, man. They took all this off my boat. Too bad for them they were so stupid that they carried along the connecting evidence."

"Al, the one guy, that ugly sonofabitch, was spying on me and Mike last night. I saw him at Bob's then later at the Sunnee Caribbee. He even made a threatening gesture, at one point."

"He probably heard us discussing our plan to spend the day out fishing."

"Do you think he could have overheard?"

"Hell, you were so loaded last night, Geoff, I'd be surprised if half the island didn't know we'd be out here today. You were trying to invite everyone along for the ride. It wouldn't have taken a mastermind spy to figure out a method to dispose of you. And they would have had my ass in the bargain."

I smiled, a wry-looking set to my mouth, but only mumbled, saying, "Sorry," realizing I'd been responsible for putting both of us in danger.

Then I considered the fact that someone thought me a threat. Possibly Pigface had killed Sarah and also tried to kill me because I was the one who'd found her body. And he could have overheard Mike and me in the bar at Lower Bay during our cack-handed attempt to investigate the murder. At least now I wouldn't have to worry about Pigface any longer, and maybe we'd inadvertently, and unknowingly, disposed of Sarah's murderer as well.

After we moved the beer and cider back over to *Suzie-Q*, and the cigarette boat was secured, ready to tow, Al set a direct course for home. Never one to miss an opportunity, he threw out the fishing lines, and we caught a couple of small tuna on the return trip.

Arriving at the main wharf in Port Elizabeth, we were met not only by the police, but also a large number of onlookers. It was almost as big a crowd as the one that appeared earlier the previous month to marvel over a seven-hundred-and-fifty-pound marlin caught by an American angler in the Bequia channel. We were big news. Maybe not as big as a large fish in this seafaring community, but we had, after all, managed to "find" and reel in some of the biggest drug runners in the country, giving the police three less things to worry about. And it was guaranteed that no one on Bequia would be mourning the deaths of these criminals—not even their mammas.

Al and I told the police the story we'd agreed upon, not introducing any unnecessary information. We'd found the boat drifting and the guys in it already dead, maybe the result of high-seas piracy or a drug deal gone sour, but we couldn't be sure. After talking with the police, they let us go.

"Sushi tonight," Al said, making the announcement to me. "Don't forget the tuna we caught on the way back."

I didn't have the heart to tell him that eating anything at all was the furthest thing from my mind at the moment, let alone sushi.

"Thanks, Al, but I think I'll skip that. It's been enough of a day already. But thanks, man—for everything, I mean." I was lucky in the extreme to have spent that day with a good friend who was not only resourceful, but could also be counted on to hold everything together in an emergency.

"Thanks for the adventure, and no problem," Al said, winking at me. I knew he meant it, too. I'd never again need to express my heartfelt gratitude to the man for what he had done. It was understood between us.

Al and I parted company at the wharf—he to look for Boney and find out what had happened to his boat and I to go back home and try to collect myself. After living for two years on this island where nothing ever happens, the past two days had been nerve-wracking, to say the least. I wasn't sure I could stand any more surprises.

In an attempt to calm down those jangled nerves and do a little quiet thinking along the way, I walked the Harbour road from Port Elizabeth to the far side of Hamilton. By the time I reached the boathouse, it was almost noon. Angie was in the kitchen, throwing together a sandwich. In spite of my still somewhat queasy stomach, I decided I'd better have something to eat, since I'd completely forgotten my packed-snack during all the excitement of our adventure. After I'd reassured her that I was okay, and that Al had managed to save both our butts, Angie made another sandwich for me while I told her of the rest of that morning's events. We have no secrets—she knows all about my past—so, in spite of my agreement with Al, I told her everything. Her face greyed again and tears appeared in her eyes.

"Geoffrey, I do not like this. What if Al is correct and his boat was sabotaged in order to get at you? This could all be connected with the murder, you know. Maybe someone did this to dispose of you, to stop you from investigating. I don't think it's a coincidence at all that they were after you this morning." She stroked my arm with a shaking hand while we both stood at the kitchen counter.

I'd been facing away from her, thinking, but after she finished speaking, I turned my head and gazed deep into her eyes, considering what more I should say, not wanting to frighten her any further.

"You could be right, Ange. I'm sure Pigface was spying on us last night. He was openly staring at me at one point. I've heard, though, he wasn't all that bright a light. So Al and I both think he was acting under orders. If that's true, and someone else is employing guys like Pigface as hit men to do their dirty work, then they are definitely serious and I'm still in great danger. I may know too much for my own good right now."

I wasn't doing a satisfactory job of reassuring myself, let alone Angie.

"The question is, who's the boss?" I asked as I pursed my lips in thought.

Ange leaned over and kissed me. "Well, I do not want to know. In any case, I don't like this one bit, Geoffrey. You have become involved in something that has absolutely nothing to do with you—or with us. Can you not tell Wilson to just sod off and find someone else to do his bidding?"

"No, Ange. The man's counting on me. I'll try to be careful and keep my eyes open, but at least it looks as though one threat has been shut down with the death of Mr. Pigface."

We talked a little longer while nibbling at our sandwiches. Then Angie remembered something and snapped her fingers.

"Ned Watson rang and asked if you could meet him later this afternoon at a bar in Lower Bay. He said he's found the man Sarah spoke with in the restaurant the other night. Apparently whoever it is wants to talk with you, but will only set up a meeting through Ned. He also told Ned he does not want the police involved." She paused. "Oh, Geoffrey. I wish you would pretend I hadn't just told you all that. Stay home. Forget about Ned and the police. Please."

I reached over and drew her into my chest, stroked her back and kissed the top of her head. "It'll be okay, Ange." I moved a step back and looked into her eyes. "I'll just go this time to see what the boy has to say. I promise. Besides, I seem to be doing most of the investigative work for the police so far, anyway, so I'll give Ned a call, see if I can reach him. Once I've organized our meeting, though, I'm going to get some shut-eye. I'm bagged. Care to join me?" I glanced at the stairs to our second-floor bedroom while drawing her towards me again, my arm around her shoulders.

"No, I have some things to do in the Harbour this afternoon, but I'm sure Gus will be more than happy to keep you company," Angie said, smiling.

Gus is an island mutt, medium sized, of Heinz 57 pedigree. He's our self-appointed protector and doorbell of sorts—that is, when he's not asleep. He followed me home one day from the Harbour, dirty, mangy, and full right through with worms, ticks, and fleas. I couldn't shake him, though, so Angie and I decided to clean him up, get him neutered, and adopt him. He's big, goofy, and loyal, and there's nothing he likes better than sleeping on our bed stretched out full-length in the crevice between our bodies. Well, he also likes to eat a lot.

I phoned Ned's hotel, leaving a message to say I would meet him at De Reef at four o'clock. Then Gus and I climbed the stairs to the bedroom and, as Angie later informed me, we were both snoring when she closed the door of the boathouse to leave for town five minutes later.

Chapter Four

I awoke from a deep sleep at around 3:00 p.m. Gus was still snoring. I shook the dog hard to wake him so he could take a quick piss-run outside the house before I left. It's sometimes difficult to make Gus understand he has a job to do, protecting the house and us. He has it lodged in his mind that we're his servants. Or maybe he has a teenager's brain and considers us parents who exist for his sole convenience. Whatever, he can be a pretty lazy dog.

I showered and changed but still had lots of time before my appointment with Ned, so I decided to walk, knowing the exercise would do me good. There's one problem about living with a beautiful woman like Angie; I feel obliged to at least make an attempt at keeping myself in shape. It's not an easy thing to do anymore at my age, especially given my deep appreciation for fine food and drink. So whenever there's opportunity to walk, I do. Besides, I knew Angie had taken the car.

It was still a hot day, but the temperature was beginning to cool down to a more comfortable level as I reached the centre of Port Elizabeth.

Few other people were out along the road. When you walk anywhere on Bequia, you run the risk of being late for appointments because you tend to know every other person you pass. People here always insist on putting down to the ground whatever it is they're carrying and then they expect you to settle in for a good, long chat, as though they haven't seen you in years.

But since Bequia runs on Island Time, keeping an appointment means showing up within an hour on either side of the agreed-upon time, anyway. I like this relaxed attitude, but Ned Watson was an American and would expect me to be punctual, arriving right on the dot of 4:00 p.m.

It was fortunate that Port Elizabeth itself was looking sleepy and deserted that afternoon, as it usually does by that time of day. The roads were even empty of the ubiquitous pack of barking dogs. Most of the daily business of shopping and banking in town is completed by noon. By three-thirty, tourists have long-since headed for the beaches, and the taxi drivers are wherever all taxi drivers seem to go whenever you need one.

The area under the almond trees, considered the heart of Port Elizabeth, is a scene of mass confusion most of the time, with taxis and other vehicles parked every which way, while their drivers attend "parliament," which involves sitting on built-in benches under the trees, discussing "poli-tricks," righting the wrongs of the country and the world.

It was a surprise to me that afternoon that no one at all was sitting under the almond trees except the Brethren, my employees.

Rastafarians refer to fellow Rastas as their brethren, whether it's one or more, so I've always used the word in the same way, referring to my workers as a collective. Besides, they like the title.

"Hey, Brethren. What's new in your world?" I said, approaching the bench.

They both looked as though they'd smoked enough weed to choke a horse. And, in all likelihood, they had. These two are experienced gardeners and terrific guys, but Rastas in general sure do love their herb, as they call it.

The Brethren and I had come to an agreement early on—they wouldn't smoke weed while working at any of the properties I manage, but what they choose to do on their own time is up to them, and they more than make up for mornings doing without by rolling up the biggest Bob Marleys I've ever seen the minute they finish work. These joints would make Cheech and Chong reconsider inhaling.

But I can't complain at all about the Brethren. They both do excellent work and, for the amount of physical labour they're willing to put into their jobs, who am I to stop them from relaxing on their own time?

They dress alike, favouring the red, green, and gold colours of Rastafarianism, and both sport long dreads reaching halfway down their backs, although the unwieldy locks are always kept tied up on their heads and hidden away under knitted tams.

"Hey, Geoff. We hears you has some trouble today with de black fish. You cool, man?" Rasta Bongo said.

"Yeah, I'm cool." I was pleased they were concerned. "I'd appreciate it if you could pass on any information you hear about anything at all, guys. I don't want you getting yourselves into trouble by asking too many questions, but please keep your ears open and let me know what's happening."

I knew there was no point telling them to keep their eyes open. I figured with the amount of weed they'd smoked they couldn't see straight anyway, so I added a warning. "Oh, and try to hold back a little on smoking the ganja, guys. I don't want you getting picked up by the police. They're probably keeping a close watch on me right now, what with everything that's happened. So they'll also be watching you. That stuff you smoke is still illegal, don't forget. I doubt any magistrate would allow religious use of illegal substances as a defence in court. I can't risk losing my two best workmen, you know."

They both nodded, their heads bobbing in unison. Rasta I-Toe said, "I and I gives t'anks, Geoff. We looks out for you and Miss Angie. No probs, man. And we watches de police. You no worry about we."

The Brethren are good men and I knew I could trust them. When I first started the business, they had come to work as a matched set and seem to do everything together, although I'm sure they draw the line at sharing the same bed. It wasn't my place, in any case, to pry into their private lives outside of work hours. I don't know if they have girlfriends now, but before moving to Bequia they both "made babies," as they call it, with girls over in St. Vincent. This act proves manhood in the West Indies, or so they say. So I have to assume they are just good friends. Since I have never fathered a child myself, I don't think they know or understand where I'm coming from, though. They seem to feel sorry for my childless state. But we do still have a good working relationship based on mutual respect. They tell me that "for an old white guy," I work "almost as good" as they do. That's supposed to be flattering, I suppose. I'm about ten years older than the two of them, so I'm not sure where they get this old guy-business, but I do take their comment as a compliment.

They're in agreement with each other on just about everything. The one point I've heard them argue was whether, as true Rastafarians, they should or should not eat "flesh," their name for all meat products. One of them does, the other doesn't. While working side by side, they've carried on lengthy and rather heated arguments about chicken eggs and whether or not the yolk could be considered flesh. It boggles the mind.

But, otherwise, they both work hard and are capable of putting in more than a full day's work, even during the hottest weather. They're also knowledgeable about tropical plants. This expertise has helped make me look good to my clients over the past two years.

"Guys, one other thing—when you've finished at the Martin house tomorrow morning, would you be able to put in a few extra hours at The Clouds, to get it ready for Mr. Wilson? He's arriving sometime this week and has enough to worry about as it is. I know the gardens are in good condition already, but I'd like the whole place to look nice for him."

"Right, Geoff. We makes it sweet. Wilson be happy," Rasta Bongo said.

"Thanks. Now I've got to get moving. I have to meet someone in Lower Bay. I was going to walk, but I'm running short of time. Maybe I should find a water taxi."

I glanced over at the shore to see if one was hanging around looking for a potential passenger. No one was there. Rasta I-Toe stood up and walked to the edge of the beach. He whistled a loud, long note then waved out to the Harbour, and a water taxi materialized, as if out of nowhere. The boat motored towards the closest jetty.

"Thanks, Ras. I'll pick you both up in the morning, like usual, to go to the Martin house. See you at seven o'clock," I said, and walked over to the jetty.

"Right, right, Geoff. We sees you, if Jah willing to spares we another day."

Their answer hit my back as I left. This is what they always say to me in parting, as opposed to a simple "goodbye." I'm not sure which one of them said it this time. They may have spoken as a duet, for all I knew.

Before I could walk to the shore's edge, someone shouted my name. I looked back down the road. Mike was walking towards the town centre from the direction of Mac's, having just finished with the Ladies' Luncheon, I guessed. Those women sure do love to talk, so their lunches often extend well into dinnertime.

"Hey, mate, I heard about your morning. You okay?" Mike said while walking up to me.

"Yeah, thanks, pal. I'll tell you about it later. I have to meet Watson in Lower Bay right now."

"If you're going to be home tonight, I might invite myself over for a sit-down on the end of your dock. I'm not sure if it's important, but I may have something of interest for you. One of the lunch ladies spoke with Sarah over the weekend. They were old friends, from when Sarah was still Mrs. Wilson."

It was just like Mike not to take long unearthing a possible connection to Sarah's murder.

"Thanks for the quick work, Mike. Yeah, Angie and I will be in tonight. You're welcome to come over any time. See you."

I left him at the road, walked back to the shore, and jumped into the water taxi. The driver backed out, turned the boat around, and left the jetty to take me to Lower Bay.

I could see Ned Watson sitting at the bar in De Reef when my taxi pulled up on the shore. I took off my sandals, paid the driver, and hopped out onto the sand as the taxi reversed and motored away. Once I was above the highwater mark of the beach, I put the sandals back on my feet and headed towards the restaurant. I looked over at the bar. Watson was glancing at his watch, still on North American time. I thought to mention that if he were interested in relaxing and enjoying what Bequia is all about, he should take off his watch, but I figured the guy had already been through enough, what with his girlfriend being murdered. Relaxation would be impossible, and the furthest thing from his mind.

No one was on the beach or in the water and Ned was alone at the bar, save for the bartender. A typical afternoon at that beach during the off-season.

"Hi, Ned," I said, as I reached his side. "Sorry if I'm a little late. I had kind of an exciting morning, to say the least." Then to the bartender I said, "Your coldest bottle of Hairoun, please." I turned back to Ned. "Can I get you something?" He held up a half-empty beer bottle and shook his head.

Once my beer was served, I suggested we move to a table off to the side where we could talk in private.

After we'd settled in our chairs, Ned said, "I asked the guy to join us at four-fifteen. I hope he can give us some solid information and isn't just jerking me along. What happened to you this morning, by the way? I heard stories. Something about you picking up a few high-seas pirates."

News travels fast on Bequia.

"There aren't still any real pirates around here, are there?"

I took a swig of my beer. "Without question," I said. "Piracy is a big problem in the Caribbean. And modern-day pirates are more dangerous than any imagined by Robert Louis Stevenson. But they're less likely to be spotted, let alone stopped, because they aren't obviously dressed, like the Johnny Depp/Jack Sparrow version in *Pirates of the Caribbean*."

"Why don't the authorities do something about them?"

How could someone live this long and still be so naïve?

"The local authorities don't have the resources, trained manpower, or equipment to fight this battle, so they *can't* catch them. The Americans, your government, come barrelling in with helicopters every once in a while. They'll spot and burn a few ganja fields then breeze out, leaving the true criminals behind, still trading hard drugs, still pirating unsuspecting yachties, all the way along the Caribbean coastline. These guys we found today had a boat that will always outrun anything the local coast guard operates. Hell, the water taxi I came in just now is faster than the coast guard boat! The local police are quite pathetic, you know. So these pirates have full control of the territory and get away with, well . . . with murder."

I bit my lip, realizing I'd just spouted off about crime to a guy whose girlfriend had been murdered. What an idiot!

Before I could cover my embarrassment by giving Ned the police version of what had happened, I was interrupted by a voice behind my back.

"So, Geoff, I hear you have been attracting several dead bodies this week. We must all be careful of how close we come to you."

I turned around. Hermut Landecker was walking towards us. An Austrian who had lived on Bequia for a number of years by then, Hermut owned Bob's. Under his management, the establishment had become somewhat successful, appealing as it did to local clientele and some down-at-heel sailors and rummies who had oftentimes found themselves shipwrecked on Bequia's shores.

Rumour had it the original Bob sold out to Hermut's first low offer then skipped the island, and his numerous other debts and obligations, one jump ahead of the creditors. Hermut had been somewhat more successful in making the bar work, the rumour being that, unlike Bob, he had financial backing from European investors or somewhere. But we'd never learned the truth, because he maintained a low-key profile, never getting involved with the rest of the expatriate community.

The gossip was that Hermut hired his staff from the poor countryside on St. Vincent, and his preference ran towards fifteen-year-old girls. It was also rumoured that one of his employment requirements was that these girls sleep with the boss. I'm not sure how true that story is, but the restaurant did have a revolving door when it came to employees, and those exiting would leave on the next ferry back home to St. Vincent either when their boss tired of them or when they discovered they were pregnant. Who knows? Perhaps there are many little half-Austrian, cream-skinned babies running around St. Vincent. The same kind of thing happened with other expats living on Bequia before Hermut arrived, and it could happen again.

Anyway, my attitude has always been one of "to each his own." I had little personal knowledge of Hermut and never drank in his bar, with the exception of the previous night, so I was surprised he recognized me at all. But then we all do tend to think we're anonymous here when the case is the exact opposite. Everyone knows every little thing there is to know about each and every one of us. Or at least they think they do. Bequia is a small place, after all.

"Oh, hello, Hermut. Actually, I wouldn't count the three bodies this morning. That was a total fluke—Al and I found the boat drifting. We were out there fishing. And I wouldn't count the woman in Wilson's pool yesterday, either, because I didn't murder her. So, all in all, I'm a pretty safe guy to know."

"Well, I still think we must be more careful. Never have we experienced so many dead people on Bequia at one time before." He turned and spoke to Ned. "You, my friend, must not sit so close to that man." Laughing, he pointed at me, then moved his finger back to point at Ned. "You might be next. But," he said, looking at me again, "I was flattered to see you in my bar last evening. It gives me pleasure to greet a new, ahhh, einen neuen Kunden . . . How do you say? Ach so—a new customer. You must come by more often."

I studied his face, not sure if I believed him. I hadn't seen him the previous night, but he seemed to know the comings and goings of his patrons.

"Ned, this is Hermut. He owns the bar and restaurant where you and Sarah . . . " My voice trailed off when I realized what I was saying, but Ned had already stuck his hand out towards Hermut, who handled it in return with a light touch.

"Hi. Ned Watson. Nice to meet you."

"Yes, well," Hermut said, contemplating the man. Then in a voice filled with disinterest, he asked, "Is this your first time on Bequia?"

"Yes, first time."

Before Ned could get out any details, I jumped into the conversation. "I wanted to ask, Hermut. Did you see Sarah the other night, when she and Ned were at your place?"

"I did not know Sarah Wilson," he said.

"Oh, okay, then," I said, and changed the subject, resorting to something of perpetual interest. "Lucky for my friend, the weather's been holding, although the island sure could use some rain."

"It is too dry for those of us who live here. But if you will excuse me now, gentlemen, I am a businessman and must get back to my establishment. It was a pleasure to meet you, Ned. I hope you enjoy the rest of your stay on the island."

Hermut extended his hand again. Ned reached over and shook it, this time with a more hearty grip than Hermut had allowed the first time.

Turning back to me, Hermut said, "And you, Geoff, you must come by and give me more of your business. Do not be a stranger." Neither of us offered to shake.

He bid us goodbye, then turned away and walked off down the beach in the direction of his bar.

I watched his progress and turned back to Ned. "Strange character," I said, more to myself.

"You said he owns that restaurant?"

"Yeah."

Ned looked crestfallen, as though the sudden reminder of his last evening with Sarah caused him to reflect. I didn't say anything, allowing him a few moments alone with his thoughts.

When he resumed, Ned said, "The restaurant was busy that night and the bar was filled, but we didn't go into the bar side. I don't remember seeing Hermut there. But I wouldn't have considered him to be the owner. I assumed the place was run by some American named Bob."

"Wait a minute! You didn't meet him when you went to the bar yesterday, with the police?"

"No. He wasn't there. The inspector left word with an employee that he wanted to speak with Hermut, though. He must have called the police. He said he knew about Sarah's murder."

"He wouldn't have had to talk to them to know about it."

Ned looked at his watch again. "It's already 4:25. I wonder where that guy is." He was sounding anxious.

I suppose I should have explained the concept of Island Time then, if only to stop him from looking at that damn watch every ten seconds. Before I could say anything, though, I noticed someone peeking at us from around the corner of the building. He looked scared. Thinking this might be our guy, I motioned for him to come out. He approached the table, casting his eyes all around and dragging his feet so as not to rush at all. I signalled to Ned that we had company.

Ned turned around to look, and said, "That's him."

"It's okay," I said, gesturing to the guy to join us. He slinked over and stood next to the table. "We're the only ones meeting you. No police, like you requested." I offered a chair and Ned asked if he wanted anything to drink.

"Yeah, t'anks, something soft," the guy said, sitting down. Ned went over to the bar.

He was short and slight, ebony-skinned with hair braided into cornrows. His fine features would have been considered sweet or pretty by island standards.

"I don't think I know you," I said, while we waited for Ned to return. "Are you from Bequia?"

"No. I name Big Fly. I from Owia."

I knew the place—a village on the north coast of the island of St. Vincent, not far from where the Brethren were born.

"I comes to Bequia long time, but I be back Owia for a couple months. I reach back Bequia just now."

"Just now" is one of those great local expressions that refers to any time from the recent past all the way into the foreseeable future.

"Ned said you wanted to talk to me about Sarah Wilson. He mentioned you spoke with her at the restaurant the other night, but he doesn't know what the two of you talked about, only that whatever you said caused her to become agitated. Can you tell me about your conversation?"

Big Fly glanced around. He was scared. The whites of his eyes showed so much that the irises had almost disappeared altogether. He said, "I tells she be careful. She in big troubles. I tells she Wilson in de same big troubles. Dey must gets test."

I didn't have a clue what he was talking about. "What kind of test? And why is Mr. Wilson in the same danger as his wife? Is someone planning to kill him as well?"

Ned joined us again, sliding a bottle of Pepsi across the table.

Big Fly took a long sip, looked me straight in the eye, shook his head and then delivered a word that packed a punch.

"AIDS," he said, point-blank.

I sank against the back of my chair. "Whoa!" was all I could manage.

AIDS has been running rampant throughout St. Vincent and the Grenadines for years and is now at almost epidemic proportions. It's said that the percentage of this country's population diagnosed with AIDS is close to Haiti's high levels which, if true, would make St. Vincent the country with the second-highest incidence of AIDS in the western hemisphere.

And the erroneous belief has always been that AIDS is a gay problem, spread within the small homosexual population—that heteros, and women in particular, are not at risk at all. Talk about burying the collective citizens' heads under a stone of wishful thinking! Also Caribbean governments and religious leaders have done little to dispel this myth. In Grenada, protests were organized to stop cruise ships carrying gay-exclusive groups from tying up at the wharf. The protestors stated that "those people" would spread AIDS as soon as they stepped on shore. So hatred for gays in this part of the world isn't just based on quoted passages from the Bible; it's due to ignorance, as well.

Then I asked, "Wait a minute, what makes you think the Wilsons might have contracted AIDS?"

Big Fly looked down at the table and said, still whispering, "Me and Sarah, we lovers."

So, this was the famous beach bum Sarah had taken up with, her partner in the public affair that led to her separation from Wilson. Big Fly was a good-looking kid, but he was no more than that—a kid. I gauged him to be about twenty-five years old, which would have put him at about twenty-three when he and Sarah were getting it on. What was Sarah thinking at the time? Was Big Fly that good a lover that she would have risked her marriage to Wilson? I was beginning to wonder if maybe the hot sun fried the brains of these middle-aged women who took up with younger local boys. Or could the sex these boys provide be that good?

"So, what makes you think Sarah could have AIDS?" Ned asked Big Fly.

"I tests positive."

"Shit!" was all I could say. Then it struck me like a brick to the side of my head. I turned to Ned and said, "You'd better make arrangements to get a test, man."

"Yeah, that thought occurred to me as well." Ned had crumpled over on his side of the table.

"I tests positive, but I no bad man. I comes to Bequia and tells all my womans, warns them. I sees Sarah by Bob's Sunday night, so I tells she so. She bawl and she bawl when I say she must gets de test, and then she go back to he." Big Fly pointed at Ned. "I tells she Wilson must gets de test. She say she call he. Then she dead. Wilson no know. Geoff, you must tells he."

I had my doubts Sarah and Wilson had resumed any normal conjugal relations after her affair with Big Fly, so I didn't think Wilson could have contracted AIDS from her, but I promised Big Fly. "I'll tell Wilson about it, as soon as I can."

Then Big Fly added, "Geoff, you is in plenty danger."

It was on the tip of my tongue to say I couldn't recall having slept with Big Fly as well. "You mean, I should be tested for AIDS?"

"No, not AIDS. Bad things happening on Bequia. Bad people. You watch," he said, pointing two fingers at his own eyes.

It seemed Angie and I weren't the only ones paranoid about my current dangerous situation.

"What kind of bad things?"

"I no can tells, but dey plenty bad. I serious. You must watch."

"Should I tell the police?"

"Dey no knows. Dey no helps. You must watch yourself. You no trust nobody."

"Thanks for the warning, Big Fly. Now, how about you? Do you need some help? What are you going to do now?"

"No, please, Geoff, I is okay. I sees my Bequia womans. I tells dey all. Now I goes back and lives in Owia. My mamma, she takes me home. I gets ready and be dead." He looked down at his folded hands resting on the table.

Unlike many Vincentians living under an AIDS death sentence, Big Fly at least had one caring family member who would look after him when he needed it most. With the stigma attached to AIDS and its victims in this country, Big Fly was one of the lucky few who wouldn't suffer in solitude.

"You keep saying 'women,' plural. And you call them your 'Bequia women'. Exactly how many women are you talking about, Big Fly, besides Sarah?" I asked.

"Just five on Bequia, few more on St. Vincent."

Geesh! More than five women who had become infected victims because of this one man.

"Uh, Big Fly," I said, hesitating, not wanting to sound preachy. "Did it ever occur to you that you should have been using condoms with all these women?" The government's safe-sex ad campaigns weren't getting through to those who needed the information most.

"Yeah, yeah. I always uses de condoms with de other womans. Plenty condoms. But condoms ruins de feeling when it be womans I loves. With them womans, I wants de loving be sweet. All de other womans, dey okay. Dey no has AIDS. I use de condoms with them."

"But out of the five Bequia women, how many did you sleep with while not using a condom?"

"All. I loves dey all," he said, giving me a matter-of-fact wave of his hand.

I shook my head in disbelief. With reasoning like Big Fly's, it was no wonder there was an AIDS epidemic in St. Vincent and the Grenadines. It wasn't that people weren't receiving enough education on the use of condoms. They were choosing to ignore what they were told. It didn't bode well for an entire generation.

"Well, Big Fly, for everyone's sake, let's hope your days of unprotected sexual activity are over." Big Fly hung his head.

How many other women could this one man have infected in such a short time? And all for the sake of a fleeting moment of pleasure—although it did sound as though Big Fly had experienced plenty of those fleeting moments.

"The offer still stands, anyway. If you need any help at all, please call. We can work something out. Do you know how to reach me?"

"Yeah, I knows you. And t'anks for dat, man, t'anks," he said, mumbling into the table. Raising his head again and looking into my eyes, he said, "You no forgets to tells Wilson?"

"No, I'll tell him. Thanks for making sure to warn Sarah. I have a feeling, though, that Wilson will be okay." I was trying to console him, but when I said that, a look of panic clouded Big Fly's face, so I was quick to add, "but I'll make sure I tell him anyway." My assurance seemed to bring relief.

Big Fly, shoving away from the table, said, "I gone," and disappeared without a sound, just like when he'd arrived a half hour earlier.

I looked over at Ned. He hadn't said a word during my conversation with Big Fly. He looked like someone who'd had the stuffing knocked out of him. And to think, a mere two days before, he'd been just another happy tourist looking forward to his holiday on Bequia with a beautiful woman.

"I wish I could go back to the States right this minute, but the police told me I can't leave the island until they say it's okay for me to go. Besides, I'd like to stay for Sarah's funeral—that is, if Wilson lets me attend."

I did feel sorry for the guy. "What are your plans for tonight?" I said, trying to figure out a way to cheer him up. "I'm honestly too beat myself after the early morning I had, otherwise I'd invite you back to my house for dinner. I wouldn't be very entertaining company, though. But you do look like you shouldn't be on your own tonight."

"Thanks for your concern, Geoff. I guess I'll go back to my hotel room. It's paid up until the end of the week, so at least I have somewhere to stay. I should be okay." He didn't sound convinced of that, looking pathetic and sorry for himself.

"I have an idea. I'll call my friends, the Hallidays, and suggest they ask you over to their place. Or, better yet, why don't you treat them to a dinner at Nando's. The food there is excellent and it's kind of a funky place. You'll like it. I know it's the Hallidays' favourite restaurant. I hate to think of you being alone tonight, and Doc and Mel would be great company. He'll answer any questions you have about HIV, and Melanie will mother you to death. You won't know what hit you, but I can guarantee after a dinner with them, you'll feel a damn sight better than you do at the moment."

I managed to receive a nod of agreement and a faint smile.

"I'll call them from the bar phone, check that they're available tonight, then I'll let you talk with Mel yourself to make arrangements."

"Thanks, Geoff. Being with someone tonight will be better than sitting alone in my hotel room. There isn't even a TV."

I didn't want to tell him that most hotel rooms on the island don't offer any of the usual amenities American tourists expect and demand. Bequia is different from other holiday destinations, but he wouldn't have known or appreciated that before coming here and experiencing it for himself.

"Then, after you go for dinner with the Hallidays, I also want you to make a point of getting out for an island tour tomorrow. You might even consider going out on a charter boat for a day sail to Mustique or the Tobago Cays. I'd rather have you return to the States with better memories of this place than the inside of a police cell."

"Okay, will do," he said. "And can you tell me if there's a gym on the island? I haven't had a workout since I arrived."

Now it seemed I was becoming Ned's tour director.

"Yeah, there's an open-air local place on the road to the airport called the Ruff Neck Gym, but the equipment is all homemade. That might not be to your liking. An American woman has set up a gym in her house, though, and I hear she has a top-of-the-line facility. It's on the way to the Hallidays' place. Ask the taxi driver to stop so you can have a look for yourself. Let me call Mel and Doc."

I made the phone call and finished organizing Ned's evening. Then we said goodbye. He pumped my hand, thanking me for my help.

I managed to wave down the one lingering water taxi in Lower Bay and asked the driver to take me all the way across the Harbour and back home to Hamilton. I was looking forward to a light dinner with Angie, a chat on the dock with Mike, and an early night to bed.

Angie and I were finishing washing the dishes when we heard the sound of Mike's dinghy engine as it approached our dock.

Angie said, "You get three chairs. I'll make coffee for the two of us and bring out a beer for Mike."

I put down the dishtowel, picked up the chairs on my way out of the boathouse, and walked down to the end of the dock to meet our friend.

"Nice night," Mike said as I came up alongside. He hopped out of the dinghy, painter in hand, and crouched over to tie up.

I tilted back my head. "Yeah, beautiful."

The sky was clear. The moon, just beginning to rise, was waxing to full, and the stars were brilliant. We sat on the chairs then settled into some amateur astronomy, just to kill time until Angie joined us. She walked down the dock five minutes later carrying a tray of coffee mugs and a couple of bottles of beer.

"You're a right Sheila, you are, Ange," Mike said, then added, "Cheers, mates."

I explained what had happened that morning out on Al's boat, but didn't tell him the full story. Even though it was Mike, I decided to protect the truth. It wasn't because I didn't trust him but because I thought it prudent Al and I stick to the story we'd concocted.

"Phew!" Mike said when I'd finished. "I'm glad I had to attend the Ladies' Luncheon and that you didn't manage to talk me into joining you. I never like meeting up with any of those drug runners, dead or alive. And Pigface? We saw him at Bob's last night. You remember? Did it occur to you and Al that those guys might have been after you?"

I wondered if Mike was seeing through my story. Trying to draw him away from the subject, I ignored his question and told him about my meeting with Big Fly.

"Oh, too right, I know the lad. He was a bartender at Bob's a while back."

"Really? I didn't know."

"Yeah, well, like all employees in that place, he didn't last long. Too bad he has AIDS, but I'm not surprised. Poor bloke."

We all considered the situation without a word out loud, then I asked, "So what information do you have, Mike?"

"Like I said earlier, this may not be important. Maybe not even accurate, but Trisha, a close friend of Sarah's, was at the lunch and said Sarah told her on Sunday she was indeed back on Bequia to gather information, maybe even for the purpose of blackmail, like Watson told you and the police. Trisha said, though, she got the impression Sarah was hoping to expose someone other than Wilson. Not that she indicated who that person might be, and Trisha didn't think to ask at the time. I don't doubt she was itching to know, though. This woman loves sinking her teeth into a good story. But she figured she'd be seeing Sarah again soon and would get the full scoop then. Unfortunately, Sarah was murdered before they were able to meet."

"Why didn't she go to the police with this information?"

"I don't think she realized it would have been interesting to them. Really, it's not much to go on. Although, I told her that, considering what little information they had, anything might be useful."

"Well, you're right and it may be something. But then again, who knows? It doesn't mean diddley squat unless we figure out who Sarah planned to blackmail, if that was even what she was here to do in the first place. Did any of the other women at the lunch know Sarah? Anyone say or know anything?"

"No. There's apparently only one other woman living on Bequia, Mary Beth, who kept in contact with her over the past couple of years, but she's off-island right now, on a walkabout, and completely out of touch. Otherwise we could have asked her. I'm sure she's been informing Sarah of everything that's gone on here since she left the island. Maybe they'd been in contact and she told Sarah something that prompted the trip to try her luck at raising the cash she needed. Hell, it didn't even have to be someone on Bequia Sarah was planning to blackmail. There are a lot of other people throughout this country with skeletons they don't want anyone knowing about, and they'd pay a lot of money to keep those hidden well away."

I had to agree on that point, having my own secrets to hide.

"Well, I don't see we're any further ahead with this," Angie said, stretching and yawning. "If you gentlemen will excuse me, I think I'm going to turn in. Don't stay out here too long. I only brought Mike two bottles of beer for good reason." She stood up, put the empty cups and bottles on the tray, picked it up, and began walking back to the house.

"Just leaving," Mike said, calling out to her back. "Goodnight, Angie, and thanks for the beer." Without turning, she raised one arm and waved at us.

Once she had disappeared into the house, Mike said, "Angie is right. Sorry, mate. I'll keep listening, though, and see what else I can turn up."

"Your detective work is much appreciated, my friend." I bowed my head towards him. "The one thing still bothering me about all of this is, if Sarah came back to blackmail someone, and people knew of her intention, then presumably the person she was going to blackmail knew as well. Maybe he's who she met with on Sunday night when Ned told us she was called out. And maybe that's who murdered her. It's possible we're dealing with someone both desperate and dangerous."

My mind flashed back to my own close encounter that morning and I shuddered. In the dark, Mike didn't notice.

"Well, no worries for any of us, really," he said. "Sarah's dead so the blackmail victim probably thinks he, or she—whatever the case may be—is now safe."

"Yeah, you're right. We don't even know if the person Sarah was planning to blackmail is a man or a woman. We really don't know much."

Mike stood up. "It's time I shoved off and let you get upstairs to your missus. I was thinking of going for a sail around Bequia tomorrow, more to get out and stretch the canvas than anything else. Care to come along?"

"It's tempting, but I'd better stay on land. I have some things to do. I still have a business to run, don't forget. We can't all live a life of leisure like you idle rich. Thanks for the invitation, though. Maybe next time." I stood up, stretched my arms to the sky to get the kink out of my back then reached down and started folding the chairs.

"Right-o then. See you later, mate. Thanks for the beer and the use of your dock," Mike said as he climbed into his dinghy. "Nice night." He gave the sky another glance before pulling the cord. Then, revving the engine, he motored back to his boat.

I waited at the end of the dock and watched as Mike made his way across the Harbour. It was a quiet night and the moon was now shrouded by cloud, so the stars in the southern sky appeared even more brilliant than they had earlier in the evening. The peacefulness of the place made it hard to imagine there could be such goings on as we'd experienced those past couple of days. Bequia was, after all, paradise. Nothing bad is ever supposed to happen in paradise.

I knew Angie's early exit from our evening's seaside chat was not due to being tired. I could sense she didn't want to hear any more about the murder or have to think about its implications. With this new information from Mike, as well as Big Fly's warning, an eerie feeling that I was in more danger than I'd first thought had lodged itself in my brain, and Angie, no doubt, was putting two and two together as well and had come to the same conclusion. I was going to have to watch my back and hope our shared apprehension was unwarranted.

Chapter Five

"Come on, let's have one more game of Plantation Owner's Wife and Garden Boy. Please?"

Propping myself up on one elbow in the bed, I looked deep into her eyes. Begging never got me far with Ange, but it was always worth a try.

"I hope you don't do this with all the housekeepers." Angie sat up next to me. Placing her hands on my shoulders, she pushed me away with a gentle touch, but one that suggested any further advances would be resisted.

"You know I only sleep with the most beautiful maids. I promise I'm telling the truth." I held up one hand and crossed my heart with the other.

Angie laughed. The two housekeepers I employ are fiftyish, oversized, and mothers to broods of children as well as grandchildren. Although both are good women and excellent housekeepers, neither is my idea of attractive. Angie knew that was the case because she'd hired the women herself.

"Besides, I'm imagining *you* in a little French maid's outfit."

"Geoffrey, get off! I'm already naked! Why do you need to fantasize me in a costume? I don't know how you managed to coerce me into this bed in the first place. We should be cleaning, not making more of a mess." Angie swung her legs over the side of the bed, attempting to get up.

We were at The Clouds, preparing the house for Wilson's arrival. Celesta and Lucella hadn't been available to do any extra work.

"Well, I must be totally irresistible then because I didn't notice much hesitation on your part when I first made a move. Besides, you should take pity on me. I've had a hard week and am under a great deal of stress. I require a whole lot of love and attention at the moment."

I reached out and turned her around to face me then batted my eyelashes.

She grinned and shoved me again, saying, "You're right barmy, you are!" But at least she laughed. "Well, I have to admit it was kind of fun." She moved again to get out of bed. "But we really should get back to work and finish cleaning this house. The Brethren will be arriving soon. What would they think of their boss if they caught him running around naked with the housekeeper?"

"They'd say their boss was one smart and lucky guy!" I shot her a full-toothed grin.

But Angie was right. We had to get back to cleaning. Using my clients' houses as shagging pads is not something I do all the time—never before that afternoon, in fact. I guess the tension of the week had got to me. Angie and I were finally alone in a place where no one would be able to find us. It was too good an opportunity to pass up. Besides, Angie is one fine-looking woman. I'm a normal red-blooded Canadian man. Who could blame me for being carried away in a moment of passion?

All the stress and activity of the week had not let up for one moment, either. Before we'd arrived at The Clouds, I'd already had another busy morning.

Wilson had phoned early that a.m. to say he would be arriving at Bequia the next afternoon. "I'm leaving my Boston office within the hour but will be in meetings in Miami for the rest of today, so you won't be able to contact me. I'll catch a flight out of Miami tomorrow and arrive in Barbados around two. Would you please arrange to have the charter plane fly me over to Bequia?"

"Okay, Mr. Wilson. I can do that. I'll call Al. Do you also want me to book a dinner reservation?"

"That would be great, Geoff. Make it for the Frangi's buffet." The Frangipani Hotel has long been famous with tourists for its Thursday BBQ buffet and jump-up (local party), with music provided by a steel band. "In fact, why don't you and Angie join me?"

I thanked Wilson and agreed to meet him around seven-thirty. Then I began updating him on the investigation into Sarah's murder.

"Ahhh, Geoff, I've had second thoughts. I'd like you to hold off. Just let the police do their work."

This caught me by surprise, to say the least. After all, it was Wilson who had so little confidence in the police in the first place.

"But . . ." I began protesting.

"No buts about it. I insist that you stay out of it now. I'm serious." His voice had turned stern.

"Okay, Mr. Wilson. You're the boss. I'll keep out." Then, remembering Big Fly's request, I said, "By the way, there is something else . . ." but stopped short and thought maybe I shouldn't bother the guy and make him sweat for two days. That information was better left until we spoke in person. "No, never mind. I'll talk with you tomorrow."

We said goodbye and I hung up the phone. It rang again before I'd taken my hand off the receiver. "Hello," I said, but my thoughts were elsewhere.

"Hey, Bequia made the morning news on CNN. Turn on your television." It was Henry, my friend and erstwhile business partner, calling from Toronto. "Apparently an American woman was murdered and found floating in a pool. The suggestion being bandied about by the TV announcers is that the US State Department should put out a travel advisory for all American citizens visiting St. Vincent and the Grenadines. They're worried this murder might have something to do with terrorists, so they're warning Americans living there to be cautious."

Oh, brother! Another knee-jerk reaction from the American government. Didn't they realize their citizens were in more danger walking out of their own hometown front doors than living on a tropical island like Bequia? And issuing a travel advisory like that, warning Americans to stay away from Bequia, would kill the already tenuous tourism industry for the upcoming season.

I hadn't been worried about media coverage exposing my situation. Local reporters are even more incompetent than the police. Reporting, both for television and radio, as well as for the weekly newspapers, consists of regurgitating government press releases. My secret identity was safe, unless the foreign press began nosing around.

"Man, that's out of line!" I said. "I know about this murder and I can tell you it definitely has nothing to do with terrorists. More likely it's a crime of passion, or maybe even mistaken identity. I found the body."

Oops! I wasn't thinking and had blurted out that last sentence. Too much information for Henry.

"You did? So what happened?" I could hear him salivating.

"Uh, forget I said that. It's all still under investigation. I don't have a clue as to what's going on and, unfortunately, neither do the police. Inept doesn't begin to describe the policing here. Just hope you never have to deal with them, for any reason. But thanks for letting me know about the CNN report. Angie's turning on the TV."

Angie had joined me in the kitchen and heard part of my conversation. I motioned to her to switch on the television, covered the phone and said, "CNN." She picked up the control and clicked over to the channel.

Henry said, "I just thought of something. With this news going international, and you being directly involved with finding the body, you'd better be especially careful not to do any interviews on camera. If reporters start asking questions, you can't afford to have your face photographed. You may have a new name, but your face is still that same adorable one to all the people you once knew. We wouldn't want anyone discovering your true identity then turning you in like on *America's Most Wanted*. You should maybe consider growing a beard as well as shaving your head." He laughed.

"Thanks a lot, Henry." Nature had beat him to that suggestion. I brushed my balding head with one hand.

I knew his concern wasn't for me. He was thinking of some of the probing questions he and our other buddies back in Canada would have to answer if my whereabouts were discovered.

He changed the subject. "How's my house?" That's Henry for you, more interested in himself than either Angie's or my well-being. "I was thinking of joining you there soon, for a week or two. How's the fishing these days?"

Henry was the last person I wanted to have hanging around, even if he was my landlord. So, just to put him off, I answered, "Yeah, sure. It would be great to see you again, Henry. Maybe you'll also plan to bring some of the money you and the boys still owe me." It was a low blow, but it worked.

"Well, business has been hopping here lately anyway," Henry said, "so, on second thought, I'm not sure when exactly I'll be able to get down there. I'll let you know, though. And about that money— we'll send it to you as soon as we can. Catch you later, buddy." He hung up before I could reply.

"What a turd!" I said to the phone. I explained to Angie about Bequia's fifteen minutes of fame in the form of TV publicity. I also mentioned Henry's warning to make a point of avoiding personal exposure. Angie is the only person anywhere I've confessed to about my chequered past. As far as everyone else is concerned, they've bought my story of being just another burned-out geologist who took early retirement. But Henry was right—the people back home who thought I had "disappeared" would recognize me, if my picture were ever circulated in connection with this case.

We went into the living room to watch the piece when it repeated. The report turned out to be fleeting, with more emphasis on the State Department's warning to avoid trouble spots such as St. Vincent and the Grenadines, in light of the sudden increase in "crimes against Americans."

"And now, back to our report on Iraq, where . . . " With that announcement, I stood up and went back to the kitchen to phone Al.

"Geoff, I'm glad you called. I was about to give you a shout and fill you in on what happened with Boney and my boat."

"I was wondering about that."

"I spent the better part of the afternoon trying to track him down. He'd gone into hiding for fear of his life, knowing he'd let me down big time. He was truly ashamed. When I finally found him, it took all the persuasion I could muster, short of threatening bodily harm, to drag the story out. You won't believe this, but those three drug runners used the biggest, fattest woman on Bequia as bait to lure Boney off my boat. She kept him busy while they sabotaged it. Boney was totally innocent and had no idea what was going on while he was with the woman. He actually thought he'd died and gone to heaven on a massive, pillowy breast—until he heard what happened to us. Now I think he's about ready to die from the guilt trip he's on—that is, if I don't kill him first myself. I always warned him those fat women would be the death of him, but I kind of envisioned it would be due to one of them suffering a heart attack while they were having sex, dying on top of him and crushing out his life."

Boney's love of fat women is well known on Bequia. And, white or black, it doesn't matter to Boney—the fatter the woman, the better, as far as he's concerned. At jump-ups, he can be seen clinging to rolls of fat, smothering his face in massive breasts. But Boney isn't alone in his love of voluminous, voluptuous women. It seems the smaller and thinner the West Indian man, the bigger and more corpulent his chosen partner.

"Don't be too hard on Boney, Al. Those guys knew to take advantage of his obsession. Maybe the woman can give us an idea who hired her, although I think I already know what her answer will be. They shouldn't present us with any more problems."

"I already thought of that. She was from St. Vincent, anyway. Boney thinks she took the first boat back yesterday morning, after she'd finished having her way with him. He doesn't remember what happened, because he'd passed out from exhaustion and ecstasy by the time she left. He's lucky he's such a valuable crewmember; otherwise I'd have half a mind to fire his ass for being a dumb shit. I keep telling him he has about as much sense as a dog chasing after a bitch in heat, but then he gets such a hangdog expression I have to feel sorry for the guy. Except for this crazy fascination for Rubenesque women, he is a good guy at heart, and usually reliable."

"Let's drop this now, Al. I don't think we should try to find her."

"Yeah, you're right. But I'd sure like to know who was behind doing that to my boat, and to us, and why."

"Maybe it was only those three guys. We have to think they were working alone and hope we're no longer in danger."

"Right you are, my man. No point in being paranoid."

"Thanks. By the way, the reason I called you in the first place was to ask for a pickup in Barbados tomorrow. Wilson is coming."

"No problemo. American Airlines, I presume?"

"Yeah, the Miami flight. He'll arrive by four o'clock."

"Hey, didn't you tell me Wilson was interested in purchasing a copper? I heard there might be one available over on St. Vincent. Care to go on a reconnaissance mission with me? I'll give my guy over there a call and get back to you."

A copper is a large, cast iron cauldron or kettle. The originals were only made of copper, so that name stuck. They were used to boil juice from sugar cane into something resembling molasses, which was then made into sugar or rum. Many of these coppers were cast in foundries in the British Isles and brought to St. Vincent during the eighteenth and nineteenth centuries to be put to use on the plantations. The name of one of those foundries, Carron, had been stamped into the edge of the coppers. Al and I discovered a company site on the Internet filled with historical photos of the original foundry.

When slavery ended in the British Caribbean, and as the days of the sugar trade drew to a close, these coppers were abandoned where they sat, being too heavy to move. In the past few years, people on St. Vincent have unearthed some to sell to foreigners for use as garden ornaments. Until the foreigners put a value on them, though, the coppers were often left out to rust or were used as water troughs for livestock or as garbage receptacles. With the new foreign interest, their price soared and local people became enterprising at selling off those family heirlooms.

Wilson had mentioned he'd be interested in buying one for his garden, if Al could find something in good condition that also came with a reasonable price.

"Sounds like a plan," I said. "Let me know." We hung up.

I was already late by then to pick up the Brethren. They were supposed to begin working at the Martin house for the morning and would join me later at The Clouds in the afternoon.

After acting as company bus driver, I returned to my house and decided to go for a quick swim off the end of our dock before eating a light breakfast. I couldn't keep putting off the inevitable. I had to get some accounting and emailing done for my business.

Property management isn't always a glamour job, and some-one has to do the office work. I'd long since given up trying to convince Angie to act as my secretary. She excused herself, claiming her mother hadn't spent a fortune on singing lessons just so she could end up filing for me. Back in Canada, I'd always had secretaries taking care of office duties, so it was yet another new skill I'd had to acquire when I set up business. I'd taught myself everything, including making my own coffee. While mine is still a cottage industry, I'm completely computerized, and it doesn't take me all that long, a few hours once a week, to catch up with most of it, including the filing.

Banking is the time-consuming part. When I finished at the house, I left to queue up in Port Elizabeth. I had business to take care of at both banks. The line-up at my own was quite long by the time I arrived, even though it was still early in the day.

As I entered the bank and walked over to join the end of the line, the place went silent. Everyone in the room turned around to stare at me.

If you're not used to it, this group stare can be disconcerting, especially for someone like me who grew up in Toronto, where we were taught not to make eye contact with anyone, let alone stare. But I've learned that Bequia people don't intend any disrespect; they're just curious. Although I didn't know all these people in the line they already knew who I was and what had happened.

The woman ahead of me in the line turned around. She was one of my neighbours, the owner of a pretty little house with a postage stamp garden that she tends with a lot of love and care. I had stopped by her house once to compliment her on that garden, and she gave me a few cuttings from the plants for transplanting.

"Good morning, Geoff," she said, nodding at me.

"Good morning, Mrs. Gregg."

In a somewhat quiet voice, she said, "De Lord bless you for what you does. We all gives t'anks you rid Bequia of dat scum." She spat out the last word, and the people surrounding us nodded their agreement and continued to stare.

"I didn't do it, Mrs. Gregg. I didn't kill them. Al and I just found their boat floating out there."

She held up her hand to stop me. "We is all grateful to you for protecting we children. De bad man like dat, dey must stop. It hurt we children. We all gives t'anks to you."

"Thank you for telling me," I said.

I looked around at the rest of the people, acknowledging them as they nodded back in agreement. They then began smiling, and one person said, "Amen." An echo rippled through the group. The woman standing at the front of the line motioned that I should go up to take her place. The rest of the people in the bank fully approved and allowed me the added honour of passing them to be served first by the next available teller. I was touched by their gesture.

When I finished my banking, I nodded thanks to everyone in the line as I walked past. They were all grinning by then, and chattering with one another like a flock of noisy grackles. The security guard at the entrance opened the door with a flourish, a wide, toothy laugh on his face as I left.

The whole episode that morning reminded me that Bequia people are for the most part good souls. After too many dealings with a few of the bad sort, I had begun losing perspective, and I was grateful for that proof that there are more Mrs. Greggs on Bequia than Pigfaces.

Other than my conversation with Henry, it had been a good morning.

Later, at The Clouds, after we'd finished our snogging, as Angie, in her quaint English phrasing likes to call it, I started making a move to get out of bed when we heard a splash. Angie and I looked at each other.

"Somebody's in the pool," I said.

"The Brethren going for a pre-work bathe?" Angie raised a questioning eyebrow.

"No, definitely not. I can guarantee it's not them." Rastas have an aversion to water. They're afraid of getting those massive dreadlocks wet, knowing they could drown from the sheer weight dragging them under.

"Come on. Get dressed and we'll see what's going on." We jumped off the bed and threw on our clothes faster than we'd ripped them off an hour before.

We couldn't see the pool from that second floor bedroom, so we ran down the stairs, out the kitchen door and down the path.

We got quite a shock—another body was floating face down. This time it was male and clothed, and I could make the identification without having to turn him over. I recognized that corn-rowed hair.

"Big Fly!"

"Bloody hell!" Angie choked and then turned away.

The other thing different about finding this body was that there was blood, gallons and gallons of blood—on the path, on the patio surrounding the pool, and in the water.

A shout of "Oy!" came from the road. The Brethren had arrived.

"Oh, shit! The guys are here. I'll run up and warn them. You'd better come with me, Ange. Are you going to be okay?"

Angie nodded an unconvincing yes, took hold of my hand, and allowed herself to be led up the path to the back of the house where we met the Brethren.

"Guys, don't go down to the pool. Something else has happened. Ange will explain. I have to phone the police again. Whatever you do, though, don't go down there, okay?"

Knowing their aversion to blood was even stronger than their aversion to water, I wanted to protect them. They both nodded without speaking.

"Did you see anyone just now on your way up the road? Walking, running, or probably in a car? Anyone at all?"

"We sees nothing," Rasta Bongo said.

The Clouds is located in a new development above Hope Bay, and the house is isolated. None of the surrounding homeowners were in residence at the moment, anyway. Whoever had killed then deposited Big Fly in Wilson's pool could have taken any of a number of paths that run down through the bush in front of the house and made an undetectable escape to either the beach or back into town. It would be impossible to find out which route they'd taken, let alone who they were.

"Okay, please stay here and look after Ange for me. I'm going to call the police."

When I returned, the Brethren were looking ill, so I diverted their attention by asking them to get started on the gardens out in front of the house. I suggested they avoid the pool area altogether by taking the walkway on the other side of the property.

I didn't want to send them away, not just yet; I needed them nearby, if only to surround myself with live bodies.

The sight in the pool was a *Texas Chainsaw Massacre* kind of gruesome. I wasn't sure even I could stop from tossing my cookies. The Brethren's reaction, if they were ever to get a look at the scene, would have involved wailing at full volume as well as vomiting. They left to get started on the garden and Angie and I went into the house to wait for the police.

This time the police arrived almost at the speed of light, their response time being less than twenty minutes. They were improving. Besides the same sergeant and constable from Monday, the police inspector and a corporal were also in attendance. There was no need for them to use police tape to mark off the area, either, as what they'd used previously was still in place.

But this time I had a more difficult job convincing them I didn't commit the murder. I couldn't blame them for being suspicious, though, what with me finding two bodies in the same pool within a couple of days of each other.

After summoning them, I'd also called Doc. As it turned out, his presence wasn't only necessary to declare Big Fly dead—he was also required to attend to the police themselves, who didn't just turn green when we pulled out the body. The constable and corporal began puking their guts out into a surrounding hedge of hibiscus. Big Fly's throat had been cut from ear to ear. It looked to have been done with a cutlass.

After Doc had sat the two men down so they could begin recovering, I whispered, "Big Fly admitted testing positive for AIDS."

"Right. Ned told me. Thanks for reminding me. The virus won't have survived outside the body that long, anyway, so anyone who has touched the blood or the body is reasonably secure. I brought along some latex gloves, though. We'd all better put them on, just to be on the safe side." He took a box out of his black medical bag and handed a pair of gloves to each of us.

About ten minutes later, the police questioned me, Angie, and the Brethren, then waited until the ambulance arrived and for the attendants to remove the body before they left the scene. As they were climbing into the car, Inspector Kydd turned and said, "Do not to try to leave de country, Geoff, and I want you to come to de station this afternoon."

To make yet another full and useless report, I thought.

When the police left, I asked, "What the hell is going on here, Doc? Is someone trying to get to me, or are all the people on this island with AIDS systematically being wiped out?" Doc gave a sympathetic shrug in reply.

"Geoffrey," Angie said, "Wilson did ask this morning that you stop investigating Sarah's murder. Maybe this was meant to be a further warning, from someone else, telling you to stay away."

"Ange, I can tell you, wholeheartedly, and I shouldn't need to remind you, either, that investigating Sarah's murder was absolutely the last thing on my mind while Big Fly's throat was being slashed. Besides, I really haven't done much investigating at all into Sarah's murder. Big Fly asked to talk to me, but he had nothing to say that might lead us to the murderer. And I doubt Wilson would have disposed of Big Fly to stop me from asking any more questions." Then I said to both of them, glancing in panic from one to the other, "Help me with this. What is going on?"

"Maybe you should lie low for awhile," Doc said. "Angie might be right and Big Fly's murder could have been an attempt to warn you off. You were one of the last people on Bequia to speak with him. He was also connected with Sarah. Wilson may even have ordered Big Fly's death as revenge for Sarah's infidelity or, possibly, for her murder, if he thought Big Fly was the one who killed her. Who knows? It's all speculation right now." He paused before adding, "The police could even be behind this."

"Are you suggesting the police are murdering people then throwing them into Wilson's pool in order to pin the murders on me?" I was incredulous. "To begin with, I don't think they have the wherewithal."

"I'm not suggesting anything, I'm throwing out possible theories," Doc said. "The police have done nothing so far to either find Sarah's murderer or even come up with a motive. Now, granted, they have managed to prove themselves totally incompetent, but police corruption is also not unheard of in this country. Come on, we've all discussed this before; why is it that we law-abiding citizens know the locations of all the crack houses, yet the places continue to operate right under the noses of the police? Coincidence? That's hard to believe, isn't it? So it is possible the police are being paid to turn their backs on this investigation as well. It's also possible they could be working on behalf of someone with a lot of power, a person who wants you out of the picture." He poked me in the shoulder to drive his point home.

Doc didn't know the whole story behind my great adventure with Al on *Suzie-Q*, but he was beginning to speculate about some sketchy details I myself could no longer deny.

"Doc, I understand what you're saying and I appreciate the warning," I said, using as much sincerity as I could muster. "For now, though, we have to count on the police to solve these murders, since Wilson told me to drop the investigation. I'm afraid we must trust them to do their jobs. Al and I have already planned a trip to St. Vincent tomorrow, anyway, so at least I'll be off Bequia and out of communication for a day. Wilson arrives in the afternoon. Maybe we can find out then why he's told me to stop investigating. I will make sure, though, that I'm totally out of the picture until he gets here."

I looked over at Angie. She stood hugging herself with tight arms and was losing the battle to control tears. I reached out and pulled her body close to my chest, whispering, "Don't worry, Ange. We'll get through this."

Once Angie had recovered somewhat, I said, "Come on inside. We should finish cleaning the house."

Doc stayed to help. While we worked, I asked him about his dinner the previous night.

"It was fine. Ned's a nice guy and I gave him a long, reassuring talk about HIV and what to do once he gets back to the States. Mel took him on an island tour today to make sure he sees everything, and she's even invited him over to our house for dinner tonight. Would you two care to join us? Mel wouldn't mind me inviting you."

"No, like you said before, I should lay low, although the thought of one of Mel's dinners is tempting. Besides, it's starting to look like Hermut might be right." I repeated the Austrian's joke about people needing to be careful about coming too close to me. It seemed I *was* a threat to the health and well-being of others. I hated that friends could suffer on my account.

"I have to work tonight, anyway. But thanks, Dave," Angie said.

We hosed down the area surrounding the pool and were closing up, getting ready to leave, when Rasta Bongo ran fast up the path as though his feet were covered in fire ants.

"Geoff, come, come. We finds something," he said, breathless, waving to me.

Angie, Doc, and I exchanged a worried glance and followed him without any questions back down the walkway. Rasta I-Toe stood over what looked to be a pile of clothes. When we came closer, we saw there was also a gun alongside.

"We finds them under de bush," Rasta I-Toe said. "We cleans de bush and chook up de ground and we finds dis." He pointed at the pile.

The Brethren had been working on a dense hedge of crotons, cleaning out and hoeing some of the soil around each of the plants, when they'd unearthed this new discovery.

"Now what do we do?" I said. "Should I call the police and tell them to come back again?"

Angie was adamant. "No! We leave these where they are. I do not want Sarah's killer to know they've been found. It might give him the idea you're still investigating the murder, Geoffrey, and we cannot take a chance that he will then have reason to take a run at you."

"Angie's right, Geoff," Doc said. "Much as I don't like withholding evidence from the police, notifying them might put you in jeopardy. Besides, I doubt knowing this will help the police solve the crime, anyway."

Everyone nodded.

"Okay, but let me see if I can do something with that gun—at least make it inoperable. Not a good idea to leave it lying around for someone to use again." I picked up the handgun from the ground, pulled my Swiss Army knife out of a pocket and, unscrewing one side of the gun's handgrip, flipped out the mainspring—a little trick I'd read about somewhere. The Brethren buried the clothes and gun back where they'd found them.

There was another half an hour's work left to do, but I told the guys they could knock off early if they wanted and finish up the next morning. They insisted on completing the area where they'd been working, though. Such conscientious employees. At least I hoped that was the case and they weren't just staying at The Clouds, passing up a ride into town, because they were afraid to drive with me.

"Guys, I turned on the pool pump to circulate the water and clean out all the blood. Please turn it off again when you come back in the morning."

"Okay, boss," they replied in unison.

Angie and I walked up to the road with Doc and then stood leaning into each other until he drove away.

Angie turned her head to look into my eyes, and said, "I'm really terribly frightened, Geoffrey."

All I could say in reply was, "So am I, Ange. So am I."

We gave each other a consoling hug, got into the car, and drove home. Angie had to sing that night; I decided to take Doc's advice and lay low. The best thing I could do was spend a nice, quiet evening, sharing dinner and a movie with my silent dog in an attempt to keep my mind off what had been happening. It would be early to bed for me, anyway, as I had to catch the six-thirty ferry to St. Vincent in the morning. That ferry schedule is one of the few things on Bequia that never adheres to Island Time.

Gus and I polished off a generous helping of what could be considered the national dish of St. Vincent and the Grenadines—chicken with rice and pigeon peas. At least my appetite hadn't been affected. Nor his. We were settling in to watch a rerun of *Star Trek*, the original series, when the phone rang. I hesitated answering at first, but then, thinking it might be Angie, picked it up.

A voice I didn't recognize said, "I know who murdered the woman."

My gulp was audible. I clicked off the television with the remote. "Who did it?"

"Oh, no," the voice said, chuckling. "You must pay me for that information."

It was a local voice but it sounded like someone who had spent time overseas. He had a distinctive Bequian lilt, but he wasn't speaking in dialect.

"I'm not going to pay you for information a concerned citizen should give freely to the police. If you know who did this, then you must tell them, not me. Besides, I'm not rich. What makes you think I could pay the amount you want?"

"Not you. The husband. He is rich enough to be able to afford what this is worth to me. I am sure he will want to solve his wife's murder. You must tell him of my offer when he arrives and allow him to decide for himself if this information is worth what I ask."

This guy was just another opportunist—the island is rife with them—who had figured out a way to cash in on someone else's misfortune. I wasn't convinced he knew who had committed the murder. Also, he only mentioned the one murder—Sarah's. Either he didn't know about the second, or thought Wilson wouldn't put the same value on information about a local boy's death. The other possibility was that two different people had committed the murders. We'd all assumed the same person murdered both. I didn't mention the second body to the caller, in case my first thought was correct.

I decided to play him along and keep him talking to see if I could figure out who he might be. "If you've got information you think Wilson might be willing to pay to hear, why don't you tell him yourself when he arrives? You seem to know he's on his way to Bequia. Why involve me at all?"

"I'm calling you first, my friend, to offer you some free advice as well. Be careful. You will be next. Now, would you like to hear what else I have to tell you?" he said, sounding pleased with himself.

I had to take a chance this guy was bluffing, just trying to extort money from a lucrative source. He might have the information, but then people on Bequia have also been known to weave tales and accuse their own family members if a feud is waged long and hard enough, and they see any opportunity to make money out of it.

"Forget it! I don't think you have a clue as to what's going on. You're just some two-bit crook who has figured out an easy way to cash in. Get lost!" I said, with a firm grip on my voice, trying not to let the fear I felt enter in.

This caused him to snap, and he began ranting at me in local dialect.

"You foreigners, you comes here, causing trouble for we! I tries to help; you no listen! You be sorry, you gets plenty licks! You foreigners must all goes home, you causing nothing but trouble for we poor Bequia people! You not born here! You no belong!"

Bingo!

I hung up the phone. His rant had clinched it. I now had an idea of my crank caller's identity. I looked up a listing in the phone book then dialled 1471, which gave me the number of that last call. The numbers matched.

I dialled, and when the same guy answered his phone, I said, "Not only do I not believe you know who murdered Sarah, but you've also just proved yourself to be incredibly stupid. Now I know who you are, Mr. Gibson!" I slammed down the receiver.

Next, I phoned the police inspector and told him what had happened. It may have been only a bogus attempt at extortion, but the inspector agreed to pick the guy up as soon as possible and question him, just in case. He also suggested I consider charging Gibson with making a threatening phone call. But I didn't want to risk jeopardizing any forthcoming information he might have if he was telling the truth, so I decided to let that idea drop—as satisfying as it might have been.

Gibson is well connected in the Bequia community. An education in the States accounted for his ability to "speak white," as they call it, when talking with me. He'd returned to Bequia to sell some inherited land and then put that money to use building up a small local empire. His wealth had not been accrued as a result of legal transactions alone, but he had never been caught or charged with any wrongdoing. And it was definite he was one Bequian who could hold a grudge and seek revenge, if so driven. A local man once told me some Bequians have "meanish ways," and this man was the perfect example of that type. In spite of his foreign education and financial success, he still had a chip on his shoulder when dealing with foreigners and was known for his rallying cry of "you not born here!" as a way of deflating and dismissing any foreign involvement in local decision making.

After I finished my call with the police inspector, I unplugged the phone, not wanting to be disturbed again. I'd missed the rest of *Star Trek* and didn't bother turning the TV on to search for something else. There was no point. Nothing could take my mind off what had happened, anyway.

Damn! The guy had said I was next! I'd already known in the back of my mind that might be the case, but I had been making a conscious effort to keep the thought as far away as I could, for Angie's sake. Now his call was forcing me to bring the fact forward for examination. Gus was still lying on the couch beside me, his head down between his paws. He looked up with big, baby-seal brown eyes, as though sensing there was a problem. At least I had his sympathy.

"Well, Gus," I said, patting his head, "I think it's better if Angie doesn't hear about this phone call tonight. It'll only worry her even more. But to tell you the truth, old boy, I'm scared shitless myself." Gus wagged his tail.

I decided there was no point in sitting and brooding about my situation. "Come on, boy. Time to go outside for a run," I said with fake enthusiasm as I got up from the couch and walked over to the door. He followed at a slow pace but then dashed past me, thinking we were both going out for a walk. I stood at the door while he nosed around, did what he had to do, then came back in. I closed up the house, left a light on for Angie, and dragged my sad-sack body upstairs to bed, followed in lockstep by Gus throughout this evening ritual.

It was impossible to turn off my mind, though, and I was still wide awake when Angie returned from work a few hours later. If I'd tried to speak with her, to tell her of the phone call, my increasing fear would have been detectable, so I pretended to be asleep. Once Angie got into bed and we were snuggled up together, I was soon off in dreamland anyway.

Chapter Six

Five-thirty seems to come earlier on Bequia than in most places, but waking up at that hour gave me enough time to shower then toss back a cup of coffee before a brisk walk to the ferry wharf in Port Elizabeth. I had my choice of two ferries, both departing from Bequia at six-thirty, on the dot.

Leave it to the Bequians: if one starts up a business that proves successful, two or more others will jump on the bandwagon and run an identical business or service. At one time there were *three* ferryboats, all owned by different companies and all leaving for Kingstown at the same time. One has since ceased operation. Once, I was foolish enough to ask why all the boats left in tandem instead of staggering service for the convenience of their passengers. The answer was simple: Bequians are accustomed to travel to St. Vincent at six-thirty.

"Ohhhhh, I see," I replied, scratching my balding head. I didn't really, but knew I'd never get a better explanation than that. Tradition is strong on this island, whether that tradition makes sense or not.

We'd seen the same sort of competition between other businesses: bakeries, Internet cafés, and specialty food shops. Right now there are two competing lunch wagons—what Al calls "de roach coach"—that cater to construction crews, and they use the exact same kind of trucks (one yellow, the other blue). The women operating the lunch wagons even have the same first name. Now that's carrying competition a little far, in my book, because then it gets downright confusing.

Eventually though, some, or all, competing businesses are forced to close, either through lack of a solid customer base or poor management, or a combination of the two. So far Bequia has managed to support both remaining ferry businesses, the Admiralty Transport Company and Bequia Express, but you can see a fierce competitive attitude every morning as loyal passengers board their choice. The boat captains then race each other to be first to arrive at the Kingstown wharf while their respective passengers cheer them on.

Sometimes these boats can really pack on passengers and cargo, too, especially if chartered for special excursions (when they tend to resemble a potential Philippine ferry disaster). But, to their credit, both companies have operated, thus far, without incident. Well, there was that one time . . . The smaller ferry was coming over from St. Vincent carrying a pickup truck loaded with cement building blocks. The sea was rough that day and the truck, which hadn't been adequately secured, shifted while the boat was manoeuvring a rather large wave. The loose truck then careened into the side of the vessel and punched a large hole in a panel. For the passengers' safety and before the ferry started taking on water, the captain decided to jettison the truck, as well as its cargo, in the middle of the Bequia channel—much to the dismay of the truck's owner. At least no lives were lost.

The ferries were relatively empty as I strolled onto the Bequia Express that Thursday morning, hoping it would continue its incident-free service to St. Vincent. I didn't need any more excitement in my life.

During the school year, many Bequia students ride the ferries daily to attend a variety of schools on the mainland. This was July, however, and the passengers that morning were commuters on their way to work, some shoppers looking to buy cheaper goods on the mainland, and others were tourists on the first leg of their journey back home after an enjoyable vacation on Bequia. I said "good morning" to a couple of people I knew then settled in for a contemplative ride.

Shortly after I sat down, however, the police inspector joined me.

"Hello, Geoff. I trust you are not planning to leave de country."

"Good morning, Inspector. I'm only going on a day trip to St. Vincent." He didn't need to hear any more details of my life.

"Good, good. I am just making sure." He wiped off a spot on the bench, sat down next to me, like we were old buddies, then leaned over to whisper, "Geoff, you will be happy to know we arrested de man who called you last night. He spent de night in jail and we are now taking him over to police headquarters in Kingstown for further questioning."

"Good work, Inspector." I attempted to sound sincere. How difficult could it have been? I'd given him all the information he required to make the arrest.

"Mr. Gibson has refused to talk, so I hope he will be persuaded by my superiors to come forward with some useful information. He is also insisting on having counsel present, but he could not reach his lawyer by telephone last night. We brought Mr. Gibson on board this morning and he is now below deck. One of my corporals is watching him." His chest was puffed out like that of a mating male mourning dove, but thankfully this was not accompanied by a bobbing head and loud calls. I turned to face away from him so he wouldn't see me roll my eyes.

It's usual for the police to transport their prisoners over to St. Vincent headquarters on the 6:30 ferry. Being kept in chains—leg irons, actually—for everyone to see adds public humiliation to the stigma of having been arrested, not unlike the old method of locking a prisoner in pillory in the village square. Most people boarding the morning boat would have had a good view of Mr. Gibson. I'll bet it was totally embarrassing for my "friend." I could only hope.

But . . . Ah! Finally! The police *were* making some progress. I almost congratulated the inspector for at last arresting someone who might be criminally involved in the case. Even if the guy didn't know anything, at least the heat was off me, for the time being. But

I held back, saying only, "Let's hope he can give you some information, Inspector."

"Oh, I do not think we will get anything of importance from Mr. Gibson. He has a reputation, you know. Once he tried to extort money from a cousin and was arrested for that as well, but de charges were dropped."

"Well, he's been a real windbag whenever I've seen him, usually yakking with the taxi drivers down by the Almond Tree."

"A what?" the inspector asked, but my answer was interrupted.

"It appears the body count on Bequia is now up to five. Who will be next, I wonder?"

Hermut Landecker loomed over the two of us like a sudden storm cloud blotting out all light. I had no idea where he had come from.

"Hello, Mr. Landecker," the inspector said.

"Good morning," Hermut replied, "but I advise you, Inspector, do not sit so close to this man. He has been attracting so many dead bodies to him. He could be dangerous." He waggled a finger at me and chortled.

The guy's sense of humour was really starting to piss me off, so I said in a menacing voice, "Perhaps it's you who should be worried about getting too close to me, Hermut. Maybe you will be number six."

"Oh, big Canadian man, I am so scared," he answered, holding his hands up in front of his face and waving them. "I am trembling like your Maple Leaf." Then, turning to the inspector, he added, "Inspector, I think you should arrest this man for making threats." He laughed at his own joke.

"Gentlemen, gentlemen. Please. This is a serious matter."

"Yeah," I said, standing up and stretching my body to its full height. "I don't appreciate the way you make fun of me—or of the situation. A woman and a boy were murdered. Have some respect, even if you can't show respect for me or the police." I waved my hand back towards the inspector.

"This is the only respect you will understand." Without any further warning and just like a schoolyard bully, Hermut wound up and punched me in the eye.

"Ahhhhh! What did you do that for?" I screamed, one hand immediately reaching up to my face. I knew enough not to retaliate—not with a police inspector standing right there.

"Mr. Landecker, please control yourself!" Inspector Kydd said. "You both must control yourselves. Please, you sit down," he pointed at me, "and you sit over there." He waved Landecker towards the boat's stern.

"Aren't you going to arrest him? He assaulted me."

"Just do not let this happen again," Kydd said, waving away Landecker and reseating himself.

"I apologize, Inspector. I will leave you now." Laughing at me again, Hermut bowed towards the inspector and walked over to the other side of the boat and out of sight.

"I want to press charges, Inspector. You can't let him get away with that. I demand he be charged."

"When we return to Bequia, then you may make a complaint. It is not really an assault. He did not draw blood."

"You weren't on the receiving end. This hurts like hell."

But the main reason I was angry was because Hermut's comments and chiding meant some people still considered me to be a suspect. I'm sure there were other equally incorrect rumours swirling around the island. Besides, the police did still suspect me, so it wasn't helping at all that Hermut was making suggestions in front of the inspector, even if what he'd said was intended as a lame joke. But when it came right down to it, Hermut really wasn't funny at all. He had a sick sense of humour, as far as I was concerned, and I didn't appreciate being the brunt of it.

"Do not worry, Geoff. I never listen to people such as that. He also likes to talk big and thinks he knows everything, like Mr. Gibson downstairs." Then he changed the subject and we spoke of trivial matters for the rest of the trip.

But I continued to fume, like an awakening volcano.

Before the ferry docked, the inspector stood up from his seat, bid me goodbye, and left. I went to the stern when the ferry finally stopped moving and, from the upper deck, watched the inspector, his prisoner, and an accompanying corporal walk off the ramp first.

Mr. Gibson was forced to run another gauntlet of jeers and taunts by the passengers and onlookers on the wharf before being safely stowed in the waiting police car.

As I was stepping down the companionway to the main deck, I spotted Al standing at ease in the adjacent parking lot. He walked over to meet me as I made my way off the boat. He had flown his plane across the Bequia Channel that morning. He would have to leave for Barbados and pick up Wilson as soon as we finished in the afternoon.

"I'll explain later what that was about," I said, pointing at the police car as it sped away.

He led me over to a truck. A local guy was leaning against it, picking his nose with an index finger. He pushed forward as we approached, wiping the hand on a pant leg, and proffered that same hand to me while Al said, "Geoff, this is Chopper. He's my main man on the mainland and suitably named to be searching for coppers. This is his truck." I looked down at the hand and threw Chopper a brisk salute instead.

Both the man and his half-ton were of dubious age and appeared to have seen better days. The truck was held together with more twine, wire, and duct tape than original parts. I was curious as to what was holding Chopper together.

"Jump in," said Al. We all climbed into the cab; Chopper sat in the driver's seat and I was in last, next to the passenger door.

"What the hell happened to your eye?" Al asked, turning to me.

"Hermut Landecker. He punched me! He started out just egging me on, then pulled a fist. He was lucky the inspector stopped me—I would've killed him if I'd had the chance."

"Hermut? That's weird. What's he got against you?"

"I think he just has a screw loose, that's all. My eye hurts like hell."

"Don't worry. It looks a lot worse than it probably feels," Al said, laughing. He settled back and glanced out the windshield. "Good news, by the way. Chopper says he knows where we can buy the kind of copper Wilson wants. It's up the leeward coast a ways."

I leaned forward to look past Al at Chopper, who flashed me a big, full-toothed grin and then threw the truck into gear. We were off. There was something about Chopper that made me nervous; the faint odour of strong rum in the cab didn't build confidence. Our designated driver must have already had a pull off the bottle, and it was only seven-thirty.

"Pull in at the High Tide," Al ordered. "I want to get a cold beer for Geoff."

I protested. "It's a bit too early for that—at least for me. I'd rather have a coffee, if it's all the same."

"Not to drink, ya idiot. For your eye. The High Tide keeps their beer as close to frozen as you'll find in this town. You can hold the iced bottle on your face to slow down the bruising and swelling."

"And I gets a rum—just a measure," Chopper said.

"No, definitely not. You stay in the truck. I'll go in and buy the beer."

We stopped just down the street from the ferry wharf and Al ran in. I was grateful for his thoughtfulness. The bottle he brought back was almost too cold to handle, but the freezing certainly had a soothing effect, and in a short while, I'd almost forgotten that Hermut had punched me.

Before our trip came to an end that day, my suspicions about Chopper were confirmed—he had a serious drinking problem. Before we left the parking lot, it would have been wise to check the bumper for the sticker that read, "I Brake for Rum Shops." Chopper seemed to have an intimate acquaintance with every one along the way, and he would ask Al if we could stop for "just a measure" whenever he sensed another on the horizon. And, let me tell you, St. Vincent does not lack for rum shops.

That truck was not meant for long-distance travel on deteriorating Vincentian roads, either. I questioned whether it was made for travel anywhere at all, but by some miracle it did manage to pass the annual registration inspection. Chopper had probably paid the traffic police to look the other way, although as long as brakes, lights, and horn are working, anything will receive a stamp of approval. In any case, we also had to keep stopping to allow the engine to cool down or for some other mechanical reason Chopper concocted. After awhile, the regular breaks became a welcome relief to my aching butt.

Chopper began timing these stops, coincidentally, with the appearance of another rum shop. While Al and I waited with the truck, Chopper would get out, shout to the shop owner, then disappear inside for a few minutes. After the third such stop, when it was apparent these weren't simply visits with old friends, Al grabbed him by the scruff of the neck, preventing him from entering the next one.

"Not so fast, Chopper. I need you more sober than drunk right now, before you forget exactly where we're going. I should probably take over the driving as it is."

"No, Al. I okay. Just dis one last measure, then no more." He held a hand over his heart.

"No, you've already had your last one for today. Now, let's get a move on. We've got enough trouble with this shit-box of a truck as it is without also having a drunk behind the wheel."

Chopper hung his head and shuffled back over to the driver's side, but Al followed him in, saying, "Shove over, doofus, and give me the key."

The keys were handed over and Chopper slithered across the seat towards my side. My look said, *No further!* He made himself as small as he could between the two of us.

With Al behind the wheel, the truck, as if by miraculous intervention, overcame all previous mechanical problems and allowed us to carry on for the rest of the distance without incident. We passed through a number of small villages along the way, and Chopper emitted faint whimpers at the sight of each rum shop. The rest of the drive up the leeward coast of St. Vincent was spectacular, in spite of the bumpy ride, so I sat back to enjoy the scenery.

Once you get out of the Kingstown area and into the countryside, things change abruptly and revert back to the old Caribbean once again. The vegetation is lush—the hillsides are covered with large plantations of bananas, coconuts, and tropical fruits and vegetables. Further north it's all dense rain forests, mountainous terrain, and treacherous, narrow coastline roads perched on the sides of cliffs high above postcard-beautiful, and deserted, black sand beaches.

A large part of the island's northern quarter is consumed by Soufriere, an active volcano. Its last eruption was in 1979, but there have been several serious rumblings since then. At four thousand feet, it attracts abundant rainfall and supports a verdant tropical rain forest year-round. The heavy precipitation, along with the lava-rich soil and steep mountainsides, creates a perfect and nearly impenetrable area suitable for growing, and hiding, marijuana. If it were legal, I'm sure the authorities would have to admit that the value of marijuana grown and shipped out of St. Vincent far surpasses everything produced by the banana industry. The American DEA came into the country many years ago in an attempt to wipe out the ganja farms, but even after all the helicopter surveillance and subsequent burning of plants, marijuana still remains a viable cash crop.

The marijuana farmers formed an association a few years back and marched on the legislature to protest this American presence. All those farmers, mostly Rastas, could have been arrested that day, but weren't. This tells me that the government of the country has never really been serious about wiping out the marijuana industry. It's either that or they believe claims that marijuana is only grown on St. Vincent for personal use. Considering how much the Brethren are capable of smoking at one sitting, it is possible that the marijuana farmers are simply supplying their own people for religious purposes in ceremonies worshiping Jah and in day-to-day life of a perpetual high, but I know this isn't the case. The number of cigarette boats running up and down the coast is ever increasing. For every large shipment of marijuana discovered and seized by the police, many more manage to get through.

And everyone claims the marijuana grown on St. Vincent is the finest in the world, but I wouldn't know. The government may be relatively lenient with the marijuana farmers and Rastas, but it's a different story for foreigners. Penalties for possession are disproportionately steep, so I've never hazarded taking a chance.

Besides, while rum is more expensive than ganja, it's still cheaper than the imported mix, plus it's legal, making alcohol a more reasonable recreational substitute.

The St. Vincent countryside people tend to have little to no daily contact with foreigners. As a result, there are no artificial attractions to lure tourists up either of the coasts and away from Kingstown or the Grenadines. What the countryside offers instead is the most breathtaking and unspoiled scenery few people have the opportunity to experience.

But the local people seem to take for granted what is in their own backyard. Do they know how lucky they are to live in such a place? Many country people consider themselves impoverished, and I suppose they are by world standards. Yet they have a wealth of spectacular views right outside their humble homes, views that foreigners spend a small fortune enjoying for only a few days at a time. But then I guess you can't eat scenery and, unless there is a tangible payoff in the form of tourist dollars, that beautiful scenery may mean nothing to those who must still eke out a substandard existence.

Lately, the Ministry of Tourism has attempted to make over the entire country and create a more palatable, generic destination to better attract those ever-elusive tourist dollars and put some of that money into the pockets of the impoverished. But I know that with any orchestrated development also comes the inevitable environmental despoilment. While I don't begrudge the local people those few extra tourism jobs being created, I also don't believe those jobs should be at the expense of ruining all this fabulous scenery. And, if history is any indication, ruined it will be—and that ruination will last forever. I hope the powers that be think twice before making any permanent mistakes, but then, promising jobs is a way of guaranteeing future votes and long-term power for any political party. So it looks as though the environment will be the eventual loser if this current trend towards wholesale development continues.

Chopper leaned forward to switch on the radio. He spun the dial and rested it when we heard an excited voice giving play-by-play commentary of a cricket match.

"Turn that shit off!" Al said.

"But it de Windies and Pakistan." Chopper complied, though, with a slow reach towards the dashboard and a look at me, requesting sympathy if not support.

I hate watching cricket, let alone listening to it on the radio, so he wouldn't find an ally on my side of the cab, but I didn't want to be as abrupt as Al, so I asked Chopper, "Do you know where cricket was first played?"

"We teach de world to play," he said, tapping his chest as though he himself had been instrumental in the game's inception.

"Well, no. Not exactly. Look, which countries field teams?"

Chopper named the majority, leaving off the most important—England.

"And Canada," I added before correcting his other omission. "My country plays cricket, too, you know."

"Nah, dey not play," he said with a sneer.

Well, granted, they don't play *well*, or at least not well enough ever to receive attention from the rest of the cricket world. I decided to take a different tack, though, getting back to the game's history. "England invented the game."

"Nah, dat not what we told."

"Of course they started playing the game there. Look—what do all the countries you listed have in common?"

Chopper scratched one ear and screwed up his face to look as though he were considering my question.

"They're all, uh, Commonwealth countries," I said, not wanting to introduce the subject of colonialism into the conversation. Chopper just shrugged his shoulders, but seemed interested. "And which country is the head of the Commonwealth? England. Cricket was invented in England, and they took the game with them into the world when they, um . . ."

Al leaned forward and looked at me. "When they took over all these poor bastards and exploited the wealth of resources they found everywhere." He addressed Chopper. "Only the US of A was wise enough to send King George packing. The rest of you have remained colonies of Mother England."

"Ahem," I glanced at a puzzled Chopper then shot a look back at Al that suggested *too much information*. "Anyway, Chopper, the Commonwealth is an association of countries that owe their love of cricket to England."

"Nah," he said, protesting again. "Windies invent cricket. Everybody say so, since de sixties, when we win so much. Dey say on de TV and radio, 'Windies! We invent cricket!'"

Ah! Now I understood his reasoning. During the sixties, the West Indies team had begun playing a more aggressive form of the game and as a result were successful in beating all their opponents. So they hadn't invented the game itself, just a new way of playing it. Some enterprising company must have used this new strategy as part of their ad campaign, attempting to boost team pride—as well as sales of their product—by emphasizing this "new" game. Chopper would have been one of many who took that claim literally. There was no point in correcting him.

"Well, it's all shit to me," Al said in disgust. "Baseball! Now there's the best sport in the world, and a helluva lot more interesting than cricket." He spat out the last word. "I'd rather watch paint dry."

I leaned forward and smiled. "In Canada, we spell baseball h-o-c-k-e-y."

Al slapped the wheel in disgust but said nothing more. With silence descending again in the cab, I turned to look out the window and began thinking of Canada. I hadn't seen a hockey game in a couple of years, not even on television.

Our company had subscribed to a private hospitality box in the Saddledome, allowing the partners season tickets to all the Calgary Flames' games.

A few years ago, I'd been away in South America, checking out a property our company was thinking of purchasing. I took a taxi from the airport directly to the office, stowed my luggage, picked up the ticket that had been left on my desk, and caught another taxi to the arena.

As I walked through the door of the private box, I heard a loud sniffing noise followed by a snort and a lot of laughter. Henry was bent over, facing away from me, but turned around when Paul said, "Hey, Bob. You're late. You missed the first period."

Henry turned as I walked over to sit down, white residue still stuck to his nose. "Hi, Bobby-boy! How's everything in South America?" he said, a silly grin on his face.

"Wipe off your nose, you idiot," I said. "It's like you're trying to get caught." I looked down at the hand offering me a rolled hundred dollar bill. "No, thanks. Put it away. What if someone comes in?"

"What?" Henry said, unrolling the money and pocketing it with the mirror and razor blade he'd been using. "You think no one else in any of those other boxes is doing the same? This is Calgary and we're all Cocaine Cowboys." He giggled without control.

The other partners in the company were there, along with three gorgeous women who looked like they were possibly high-priced call girls. Knowing Henry, of course they were. I shook my head in disgust at everyone.

"Oh, come on, Bob. Loosen up. The Flames are winning. And I just came back from a Caribbean vacation where I bought some property. Nice little island called Bequia." He turned to Paul. "Hey, get Bob a drink, will you? Ask one of the girls out there to come in and take our order." Paul stood up and walked out the door.

"Come and sit here," Henry said, patting the seat next to him. "Tell me all about your trip and I'll tell you about mine."

I considered walking out but decided to stay on. I had too much of a stake in the company, and these were my lifelong friends. They had always been indiscreet about their love of recreational drugs, a love I didn't share, but they were a good bunch of guys, for the most part.

"I'll get the report to you tomorrow, at our meeting. So tell me about this island. I've never heard of it before."

"It's a nice little place, totally off the radar. There were rumours of a new airport being built, so I bought this property for a song. Managed to get in there before the prices begin going up. Nice house, with a boathouse. Lots of possibility for business there, too."

"Oh," I said, brightening up. "Did you see some geological surveys?"

Paul had come back into the box and joined Henry in laughing at my comment. "Not that kind of business," Paul said. "We're thinking of diversifying." He waved his hand over the table where the two of them had been snorting coke. "Henry's got it all figured out. We'll talk about it tomorrow at the meeting."

"Yeah, Bob. Don't look so worried. I've got it figured out. We're going to make millions, man." He patted my shoulder. "Here's our drinks." A uniformed woman walked in carrying a tray of glasses. "Now, let's enjoy the rest of this game. Go Flames!"

I must have drifted off. Al made an abrupt right turn that jolted me awake. Then we were driving up a road narrower than the main one we'd been on. We climbed into the mountainous area, up the side of the volcano. I prayed to myself that the truck's numerous patch jobs would hold together because the road looked as though it had seen few vehicles over the past decade. We'd never be able to get the truck towed out if it broke down. I turned my head and looked over my shoulder through the back window. We'd already lost sight of the ocean, the surrounding forest was so dense. I didn't have a clue where we were.

Chopper pointed ahead and Al pulled onto another side road that could have been a driveway at one time. Possibly the entrance to an old abandoned plantation, it was lined on either side by tall and stately, but very old coconut palms, some of them broken, others as high as ninety feet. We drove into a small clearing and Al stopped the truck when Chopper held up a hand.

"We walks from here," he said.

We tumbled out, grateful to be done with the clanking and clunking truck for awhile, and followed Chopper up a path. What we hadn't been able to see from the clearing where we'd left the truck were the crumbled ruins of the main plantation house, almost completely overgrown by the ever-encroaching vegetation. We walked past. From what was left, the structure looked like it must have been a massive stone house in its day.

Then a voice called "Oy, Chopper" from ahead of us. A large Rasta man stepped out from behind the ruins.

"Dis Jolly Boy," Chopper said. "He have de copper for to sell."

Whether Jolly Boy actually owned the copper he was selling or even the land we were standing on were moot points. No one else seemed to have laid claim to the place lately. Besides, he was an enormous, brawny man, not one to be questioned.

He led us a little further into the bush behind the old house. Jolly Boy stopped next to an area denser than the rest, reached down and began pulling at some vines. We all helped, uncovering what proved to be an excellent copper. Forged in the original metal, it was eighteen feet in width and still in almost factory condition, a fact that was surprising considering the copper had probably sat on that same spot for about a century and a half.

Al asked Jolly Boy, "How much?"

Jolly Boy reached down to grab his crotch, shifting the equipment there with a thoughtful look on his face, as though the action would help him consider his reply more clearly. This unconscious act of pocket pool—without the benefit of hidden hands—is something quite common among Caribbean men. Angie finds it gross, and has threatened to Lorena-Bobitt my penis *and* balls if she ever catches me at it.

"Five thousand," Jolly Boy said.

"EC?" asked Al. East Caribbean currency is permanently pegged at $2.68 to one US dollar.

Jolly Boy threw his head back and gave a big, full-belly laugh. "Ha! Ha! Ha!" His wide-open mouth displayed a couple of gold teeth. Then he turned serious and answered, "US."

Al didn't laugh. Spinning around, he whacked Chopper with

the back of his hand. Taken by surprise, Chopper covered his head with his arms after the fact and cringed.

"Are you crazy?" Al yelled. "You dragged us all the way out to this gawd-forsaken place to look at a copper that's," Al counted on his fingers, one at a time, "A, five times more expensive than my top price; B, bigger than we needed; and C, impossible to get onto your truck from where it's sitting. Did it ever occur to you that that thing probably weighs two tons? We'd need a crane to lift it; that is, presuming we could get a crane up here in the first place. Then there's the problem of walking the crane all the way back to where you parked the truck, not to mention the definite possibility your truck would collapse under the weight of this copper. And, besides all that, Jolly Boy certainly doesn't look to me like he's interested in negotiating the price down to what I'm willing to pay."

Jolly Boy didn't look amused at the prospect of losing such a lucrative sale. All of a sudden, he wasn't jolly at all.

"I no bargain with you," he sneered at Al. "There be plenty white man pays me five thousand US, maybe more."

"Sure, there's a sucker born every minute," Al replied. "But I'm not one of them. You can sell it to one of those other white men and see if he can move it out of here."

Al marched off towards the truck. I followed close behind, not wanting to stick around to test the extent of Jolly Boy's anger. His rant had begun, just as West Indians resort to when wronged, and it was all aimed at Al's back. At least, a rant was what it sounded like. Except for the word "fucking," which always seems to come through loud and clear, no matter how incomprehensible the rest of the speech happens to be, I couldn't understand a single other word, but nothing he shouted gave the suggestion we were to "have a nice day."

Al and I got into the cab of the truck, Al behind the wheel from the start this time. Chopper slinked up to the window on the driver's side.

Al said, "I should leave you here and let you make your own way home, you crazy rummy. But get in. I need you to help stick this truck together if it starts rattling apart." Al was beginning to sound like Humphrey Bogart's character, Harry Morgan, berating his al-coholic sidekick, Walter Brennan's Eddie, in *To Have and Have Not*.

Chopper moped around the front of the truck and crawled in beside me. He hugged the door, giving me wide berth. Al leaned for-ward and looked around me at him.

"By the way, out of interest, exactly what were you planning to pocket for yourself on that deal?"

Chopper gasped, "Al, I no makes no money on dat. I only makes what you gives to me."

"I doubt it. I'll bet you just lost two thousand US. And it serves you right for being so stupid, bringing us all the way up here to show us something we can't possibly have in the first place. All you'll get from me now is money for the gas we've used, like we agreed. You won't get the finder's fee I would have paid if you hadn't been so stupid and had shown us something we could've bought in the first place." Al's attention went back to the steering wheel. He turned the key in the ignition and, under his breath, said, "Dumb shit!" then focused on getting us out of that driveway, back to the main road and into Kingstown again.

Chopper melted into the seat, sullen and gazing out the front window. He didn't say another word for the rest of the drive. If it hadn't been for the stale alcohol smell emanating from his side of the cab, we wouldn't have known he was still there.

It was a good hour or more before we started getting close to Kings-town. Al and I had spoken little and only to each other. Chopper had been snoring and I was beginning to doze off myself when Al burst out with, "Eureka!" He made a quick left exit off the main road, jos-tling Chopper awake and causing him to slam into me.

"Hey, watch it, Al," I said, pushing Chopper back to his own space.

"Sorry, guys. We have to stop here."

"What's up?" I asked.

Al pulled over and parked in front of a tiny house. "I saw a copper by this place."

I looked around. Beside the house was what appeared to be more of a garbage dump than a copper, but it was definitely a copper under all that debris, and one about the size we needed. Al got out of the truck to search for the owner of the house.

"We might as well get out and stretch," I said to Chopper. He opened the door to release us and we stood by the truck to wait.

Al walked around to the back of the house but soon came out of the front door with a small, elderly woman. She looked to be in her eighties and walked stooped and slow, but when Al pointed at the copper and said, "We want to buy it," she straitened up to stand at attention.

Al is not tall, but he towered over the woman. Unaffected by his size, she looked up at him with face screwed-up, her chin jutted out. Poking him in the chest with one finger, she asked, "What you wants with my copper?"

"We'll take it off your hands, Tantie. It doesn't look like it's being used."

"You not going to t'ief a old woman now?" She looked at Al in a menacing way, as though warning she'd contend with him in a physical manner if he were out to cheat her.

"No, Tantie, I promise to pay you a fair price. How does two thousand dollars sound to you?"

Her face broke into a smile, pleased with this sudden windfall. "You takes it away today? And you pays me cash?"

Al agreed to her terms. He wasn't cheating the woman. In fact, he'd put a high value on something that had only been taking up space for her. She brightened even further, figuring she was the one getting the best deal.

"Dis house and de lands, dey belongs long time to Granny and Grampy. Dey leaves it to me mummy. I remembers long time de copper being used to boils de sugar when I only be dis big." She held out her hand two feet below her current height. "But it no used since then."

Like the copper we saw previously, this one had also sat in the same resting spot for well over a century. Now the owner would be able to use the new-found money for something useful, like a television and dining room suite.

Al asked, "Are there any men close by we could recruit? We'll need help loading this on the truck."

The woman pointed down the road. "There be a rum shop just by de next house."

Al looked over at Chopper, whose eyes had lit up when he heard the words "rum shop." Al said sternly, "I'll go," wiping the hopeful look from Chopper's face.

Al left Chopper and me to clean all the garbage out of the copper. I asked the woman if she had a shovel we could borrow. She didn't, so I picked up a dead palm frond from the ground and Chopper used his hands.

Al returned a few minutes later with five men who had obviously been drinking but were still able to walk under their own steam. A small crowd of out-and-out drunks and a few women and children followed. We had become an event and everyone wanted to watch. Al backed the truck up as close as he could to the copper while three of the men shouted directions, West Indian-style.

"Back! Back! Back!" they directed, waving him on. Then suddenly, they all held up their hands, signalling he should brake, and screamed, "Stop! Stop!"

There were two hardwood planks in the back of the truck to use as ramps; we set them up. Then we eight still-able-bodied placed ourselves around the copper and, in a coordinated effort, lifted it onto the base of the planks and began easing the copper up towards the bed of the truck.

An intense pain shot through my right hand and I jerked back that arm. I'd sliced the side of it on the sharp edge of the copper while changing my grip. Blood began first seeping then gushing out of the cut. Shock—at the immediate sight of brilliant red where it shouldn't have been—set in, kind of temporarily numbing the pain. Out of instinct, I clasped my other hand over the injured one, enclosing the cut area with pressure, and lifted both arms high above my head.

Al shouted for everyone else to stop and rest the copper. He turned around, grabbed a half-empty bottle of strong rum from one of the spectators, told me to hold the cut side of my hand upright, and then doused it with the rum. I winced with the renewed pain and even thought I might pass out but managed to contain myself in front of the crowd. The real scream came from Chopper as he watched the strong rum drip from my hand onto the ground. His barn owl-screech soon became a girlie-whimpering.

"Keep quiet, Chopper!" Al shouted, then, turning to the others, said, "Okay now, let's finish getting this thing on the truck. And watch out for the sharp edges." He looked back at me and said, "Sorry I didn't warn you about that. The edges of these things can be dangerous. You should probably sit this out. That rum will have killed any infection in the cut."

The pain was so excruciating I hadn't given a thought to infection. Things grow fast in this climate, especially infections. Al had used rum because it makes the best disinfectant and is readily available, so basic first aid is never far away. That particular rum, marketed under the label "Very Strong"—in itself an understatement—is almost pure alcohol. In fact, it works so well as a disinfectant, it kind of makes you wonder what it must do to the stomachs and intestinal tracts of the men who constantly drink it.

Chopper and a couple of the other men had climbed onto the bed of the truck and were guiding the copper in while the rest of the men on the ground and the ramps gave it one last heave. The copper was balanced on the truck bed when Chopper let out a blood-curdling scream and started wailing. This time, he sounded something like a cat caught in a blender.

"Chopper, I'm not giving you any more rum until we have this copper on the ferry, and that's final!" Al said.

Instead of quietening Chopper, that made him wail all the more. He stood there gripping one hand under his armpit.

"I think he's really hurt himself, Al," I said, and hopped onto the back of the truck. As firm as I could, I said, "Chopper, hold out your hand and let me take a look."

Chopper's wailing was down to a whimper again at that point. He showed me his hand.

In spite of all the blood, I could see his cut was far worse than mine. It was long and deep, clear through the fleshy part between his thumb and index finger.

"Stitches," I shouted down to Al. He gave me a quick nod, paid the woman her two thousand dollars, paid the men for helping us, then climbed into the driver's seat. Meanwhile, I helped Chopper off the truck bed and locked the back gate into place. The woman had gone into the house and brought out some rags. She helped me wrap them around Chopper's hand. My cut wasn't that bad after all, so I didn't bother covering it. Chopper and I were getting into the cab when another man ran up to the crowd and began yelling at us.

"Where you goes with my copper? Dat no belong to she! Dat on my land! Dat my copper. You must pays me for dat!" His voice increased in volume with every sentence.

The woman shouted, "Nephew, dat my copper and I sells it to these white man. My mammy gives dat to me along with dis house and de lands when she die. You too young to knows for true!"

"Tantie, my mammy tells we Grammie give to she. It on our side of de family. Dat money you gets, it belong to I and I. You must gives it over now," he shouted, straightening up to his full size and dwarfing the old woman.

Al leaned over to me and said, "Let's get the fuck out of here." He put the truck into gear.

When the nephew realized we were leaving with the copper, he ran up to the truck screaming at the top of his voice. "You white man, you t'ieves we heritage. Makes for de black man to suffer. I reports you to de government. De government must sends you back where you belongs so you no t'ief from we no more," he raved.

Al pulled away while the guy was still shouting. I turned to look out the back window of the cab just as the old woman picked up a large stick. She chased her nephew around the yard with it, screaming, "I gives you licks like your mammy never done for you."

When we were driving on the main road again and out of sight of the house, we heaved a collective sigh of relief. No doubt that eighty-year-old woman would eventually win the fight with her nephew and retain all the money she'd made selling her copper.

After a few minutes, Al said to Chopper, "I'm taking you to the Maryfield. It's close and we'll be able to get your hand fixed up as soon as possible."

Chopper gasped. "Not de Maryfield! Dat de pay hospital! I goes to de free hospital."

We were closer to the privately run business where patients must pay for all services. The government-run Kingstown General attends to the needs of their patients for free, or at least through a national medical system. However, the facilities are limited and its reputation for successfully administering quality health care is not good. We've heard many horror stories about patients who entered its doors and came out sicker than when they went in.

"Okay, it's your funeral," Al replied. "There's probably good reason though for that graveyard being located right next door. Lucky for you if you do die while you're in there. You won't have far to go."

About twenty minutes later, we pulled up in front of the hospital and Al told Chopper to go in through the emergency entrance. Al and I then headed across the street and into a little snackette for some much-needed sustenance while we waited for Chopper. We were settling down at a corner table to a couple of soft drinks while waiting for our beef rotis to be prepared when we heard a familiar voice at the counter.

"Two plasters and a measure of strong rum," Chopper said. He was asking the bartender for bandages instead of waiting to get the stitches he required. He hadn't seen us sitting there.

Without any hesitation, Al shouted, "Get back over!" He jumped up from the table, grabbed Chopper, and frogmarched him across the street.

While they were gone, the bartender set the rotis on the table. I asked him to take back Al's to be kept warm and ate mine in solitude. Then I took some time to examine the cut on my hand. It wasn't that bad and the rum seemed to have done the trick in cleaning it out. I'd have to make sure I looked after it, though, once I got back home.

In about half an hour, Al joined me and tossed over a few Band-Aids. Chopper slinked in moments later and sat at a table by the bar, as far from us as possible. Al turned back to the bartender, pointed at Chopper, and said, "Give him his rum. But only one measure for medicinal purposes. And you'd better give him something to eat while you're at it to help soak up all the rum he already has in his stomach. Put his lunch and drink on my bill."

I got to work doctoring my hand. My blackened eye had long since stopped throbbing, and that pain was replaced by the new pain in my hand.

Al passed a couple of Aspirin across the table to me and chuckled as he got down to eating his own lunch. "This was funny. Chopper started hitting on the nurse. He was trying to be sweet, making suggestive remarks, asking her out while she stitched him up. Big mistake. She's religious and was not at all amused, so she made sure she put those stitches in good and tight." He motioned at how hard she must have been pulling them through Chopper's hand.

While we took a rest after eating, just to kill time before I had to catch the late-afternoon ferry to Bequia, I decided to pay back Al for having bored me, telling his life story and love affair with Suzie so many times. Like most Americans, Al enjoys telling you everything about himself, so there's a game I love to play, with him and other Americans, just for the purpose of sweet revenge. I find it pretty funny, mainly because it really gets Al's goat.

"Hey, Al, did you know that Michael J. Fox is a Canadian?"

Nothing riles Americans more than Canadians listing compatriots who have made it big in the US. Al rose to the bait. He had been leaning his chair-back against the wall of the snackette, eyes closed. When I spoke, he set the chair upright and looked over at me, incredulous.

"What is it with you Canadians? You're always pointing out other more-successful Canadians. Is it that there are so few of you who become important that the rest of you have an inferiority complex? And you all do it. I swear, the minute a Canadian gets on my plane and finds out I'm American, they have to name some famous Canadian living in New York."

"And John Candy, and Captain Kirk, and Superman's girlfriend, and John Kenneth Galbraith, and Morley Safer," I quickly added, rubbing it in a bit more, laughing at him.

"Morley Safer, too?" he asked, surprised. "You mean the guy on *60 Minutes*?"

I always make a point of adding a new name each time I play, just to catch Al.

"Yeah, the same guy. I think he went to my high school in Toronto." I threw that in for the extra personal connection to fame.

"Oh, you mean you both went to the same high school at different times together," Al said with a sarcastic tone. "How nice for you. You *nice* Canadians always like to stick together, don't you?" With that, Al kicked his chair back and leaned against the wall again, ignoring my continuing laughter.

Then Chopper called over from the other side of the room. "You says you from Toronto?"

"Well, yes . . ." I said, hesitating, not sure where this conversation would lead.

"I has a cousin in Toronto. Maybe you knows he. He name Ollivierre. He have a house in Scarborough."

Chopper looked hopeful I would say I had actually met his relative and that I was even pals with him, but Al began hooting with laughter before I could answer.

With more Vincentian nationals now living abroad than in the country itself, it's likely those left on the islands have numerous relatives residing in most major cities in North America and England. But Vincentians who stayed put don't have a clear concept of the actual size of the outside world, so they think it possible their cousins, brothers, or a parent in Toronto have met every Canadian who visits St. Vincent. Since Al was laughing at me, Chopper seemed relieved that, for a change, he wasn't the butt of that biting sense of humour, although he probably didn't understand why the joke was suddenly on me. It was my own fault for trying to brag about my Canadian heritage in the first place.

Al was still laughing to himself as we drove down to the ferry wharf. He parked the truck close to the boat ramp and commandeered some men idly standing around to help get the copper on the ferry. Then Al paid Chopper, said goodbye to me, and hailed a taxi for the drive out to the airport. I shook Chopper's good hand, noting with relief that it wasn't the one I'd seen him picking his nose with earlier in the day, then said goodbye. He pulled himself into the truck cab and sat there for awhile, probably trying to figure out how he was going to shift gears using his injured hand.

It had been quite a day, all in all. I was beginning to think every day with Al had the potential of turning into an adventure. But I did have him to thank for a day so eventful it had managed to take my mind off my own recent concerns for a while.

I was exhausted and knew I wouldn't have any trouble sleeping for part of the trip home. I walked onto the ferry, went up to the top deck, found a seat that allowed some privacy, and settled in for the hour-long ride. I had to meet Wilson for dinner, but at least there was the good news of the copper purchase. I hoped that would please him.

Chapter Seven

As the ferry entered the Harbour, it dawned on me I hadn't made arrangements to have the copper picked up and delivered to Wilson's house. Organizing that would make me late for dinner. As we got close to shore, I spotted Rasta Blocksman standing beside his truck on the wharf. Blocks, as he's known to his friends and clients, is a building contractor on Bequia. I'd previously subcontracted out to him some small projects at the properties, so we had a good working relationship.

"Hi, Blocks," I said when I got off the ferry. "I have a job for you right now if your truck is available. We'll need a few extra men. I have to remove that copper," I jerked my thumb back at the boat's cargo area, "then deliver it to a house in Hope."

"No problem, Geoff. I just here picking up a small package from de boat. I gets my guys and we takes care of it for you. But I can't deliver de copper to de house until morning. Dat be soon enough?"

"Yeah, that's perfect, as long as you don't mind leaving it on the back of your truck overnight. At least there's no worry someone might t'ieve it."

We laughed at the thought of anyone trying to make off with Wilson's copper, although we knew that the possibility couldn't be ruled out—many items, some a great deal larger, have been *borrowed* before.

"How you gets de eye? And your hand? What you does, man? You be in a brawl in Town?"

"No, it's a long story," I said, sighing, having forgotten how I must have looked. I changed the subject back. "I don't have enough money on me right now to pay you for the job. Let me know how much I owe and I'll see you get paid right away."

"I knows you is good for it. You just gives me something for de guys. De use of my truck is free." When I began to protest, he added, "No, no. I serious! I hears you has a rough week. You deserves something nice for a change. Besides, you done plenty for me in de past. I be happy if you keeps de jobs coming my way."

Blocks is one person definitely devoid of meanish ways. Bequia-born, he learned the construction trade in Trinidad at an early age and now runs a successful business. He's built many foreign-owned houses on the island and always treats his clients with honesty, presenting them in the end with a quality product.

"Thanks, Blocks, I appreciate it. Remind me some day to tell you about how we got this copper. It'll be a good story to go with a beer."

Blocks threw his head back and laughed. "I looks forward to that! I takes care of de copper now. Don't you worry. Where it go tomorrow?"

"You know Wilson's house? The Clouds."

"De one where there be murders? I not have any trouble finding men to take de copper there. Everyone want to look! You goes now. I takes care of everything."

"Thanks, man."

I decided to splurge and catch a taxi back to my house. Even after having spent most of the day bouncing around in Chopper's truck, I was tired and couldn't face the walk home. I'd use the extra time I'd gain getting ready for dinner. I was also anxious to see Angie as soon as possible and tell her about my day on St. Vincent.

So it was with extreme disappointment that I arrived at the boathouse and discovered Angie wasn't there. Our car was parked in the driveway and Gus had been locked inside the house. This was unusual; we leave him outside to watch the property whenever we're out. "Where's Angie, boy?" I said as he ran past me out the door.

There was a note on the kitchen counter telling me she had gone to a hen party and would meet me later at the restaurant. A hen party? I couldn't figure out what she meant by that. Ange isn't in the habit of meeting friends for tea, in spite of her English background. The note seemed odd because her writing is always more formal, beginning with "Dear Geoffrey," then ending with "Love, Angie." It has always been kind of a joke between us. She claims it reflects her proper British upbringing. This note, with no salutation at all, was simply signed "A."

I dialled the Hallidays' number to see if Melanie knew anything.

"No, Geoff, I haven't heard from Angie all day. Maybe Suzie knows where she is."

"Thanks, Mel. I'll call her next."

"Ask Angie to phone me when you do track her down."

"I will. Goodbye." I pushed down the button to end the call and was about to dial Suzie's number when the phone rang.

"Yo, Geoff, I'm having a full moon party on Saturday night. I hope you and Angie can come out to Moonhole to join us." It was Henri-Alfred, a retired French Canadian and self-styled caveman. He likes to think of himself as the oldest-living, still-practicing hippie. Now in his seventies, he was too busy during the original summer of love trying to be a good husband and father so had been unable to indulge at that time. But, since moving to Bequia, he has more than made up for those lost pleasures by living out his fantasies at the end of the island in an area known as Moonhole.

The original concept for Moonhole was the brainchild of an American a few decades back. He envisioned houses built into, and out of, surrounding available materials of rock and stone, with a few age-bleached whalebones thrown in for good measure. The houses were designed with no square corners or conventional closed doors or windows, leaving them open to the elements. The first house was built for himself and his wife and the project evolved to include houses for friends, until the area became a community wholly owned by foreigners, mostly non-residents.

Moonhole is difficult to describe. Of architectural interest, it was a builder's challenge, and does not suit all tastes. But as far as housing developments go, it is unique. Recently it's become a tourist attraction and there are organized guided tours of the houses.

Henri-Alfred sailed into Bequia a number of years back, shortly after one of the Moonhole houses was built. He bought it on the spot, with retirement in mind. However, his wife had not accompanied him on that first trip, so when she did arrive, she took one look at the house and made a hasty retreat. They divorced soon after and she now lives in a more civilized place. A Flintstone existence was not her idea of a dream retirement.

But I have to hand it to Henri-Alfred: since his divorce, he's put together a pretty romantic bachelor pad. And he always manages to attract women wanting to share it—at least for a brief while. These full moon parties he throws every month are his way of introducing the latest babe to friends.

"I'm not sure if we'll be able to make it on Saturday," I said. "It's been a busy week. I'll let you know, though, if we do decide to go, and we'll be sure to bring ice." Moonhole has no electricity and Henri-Alfred generates only a small amount using wind power, so he can never keep enough ice to supply his parties.

"Thanks, Geoff. That's exactly what I was going to ask. Don't forget to pass the word around to everybody."

"I won't." The evening would be a good diversion for Ned. I'd have to remember to include him. Full moon parties are open to anyone, as long as they bring food and drink.

"I've got to get off the phone, Henri-Alfred. I'm getting ready to meet someone, so I can't talk right now. I hope to see you Saturday. Then I'll fill you in on what's been happening."

With a serious tone, Henri-Alfred said, "I heard you've had some trouble. I'll look forward to hearing the truth about it from you." Then his voice lightened up. "And you'll be able to meet Debbie on Saturday. She's from Miami. I met her in an airport lounge last year and invited her down. She's a knockout! You'll like her."

I had to give the man credit for still being able to attract younger women. I hope when I finally reach Henri-Alfred's age, I have similar success. In the meantime, I'll console myself with Angie. But where was she?

"Yeah, great. I'm looking forward to that. But I do have to go. Goodbye," I said, and hung up the phone.

I decided to hold off contacting Suzie. No doubt, Angie would meet me later at the Frangi, as she'd said in her note. I was probably reading more into her message than was necessary. Besides, with that independent streak of hers, Angie would abhor that I was concerned at all. If she had changed her mind and chose not to join Wilson and me that evening, for whatever reason, there wasn't much I could do to make her change it back.

I whistled Gus into the house and fed him. Then after showering and changing, I shooed him outside again, locked the door, and drove to the hotel.

Wilson was sitting alone at the bar, looking lost in thought while fondling a glass of amber liquid. He appeared to be tired and even gaunt, seeming older now than his sixty years, and thinner than I'd remembered him being the last time we'd met. But he was happy to see me. When I called his name, his face brightened as he swivelled around.

"Where's Angie?" Wilson asked.

"I wish I knew. I thought I might find her here. I was in St. Vincent all day. She left a note saying she'd meet us. It's not like her to be late for anything."

"Nor you. You're right on time, as usual. She'll turn up. But this will give us a private moment to cover business that probably would have bored her. What will you have to drink?" Wilson waved over the bartender and I placed my order for an R&C. "What happened to your eye?"

"Oh, just an altercation with an idiot on the ferry. Not as bad as the cut on my hand." I held up the bandaged appendage.

"You should look after yourself, Geoff. Sounds as though you've had a rough day."

"You don't know the half of what's been happening." I shook my head.

We exchanged small talk and finished our drinks before a waitress came from the restaurant side to tell us our table was ready.

The Frangipani, located directly on the waterfront of Admiralty Bay along the Belmont Walkway, is the oldest hotel and offers the best place on Bequia to enjoy a drink. Everyone shortens its name to the Frangi. Originally, the main building was the family home of a former prime minister of St. Vincent and the Grenadines. He saw a perfect opportunity and converted the house into a hotel. Now retired from political life, he spends most days chatting with dining room and bar guests or relaxing in one of the patio chairs that face the sea.

Over the years, the hotel has become a hub for most of the island's social activities, especially during the annual Bequia Easter Regatta, when it serves as race headquarters. And on New Year's Eve, or Old Year's Night as they call it locally, the entire island seems to be drinking at the hotel's bar, celebrating midnight. A great meeting place, their Thursday evening buffet dinner and jump-up attracts tourists and locals alike with good food, lively music, and dancing.

Hotel entertainment wasn't on our minds that evening, though, as we helped ourselves to the buffet of grilled steak, chicken, fish, assorted salads (including breadfruit, a Caribbean favourite), local vegetables, and a side table of desserts. We sat down to eat.

"We found a copper for you today, Mr. Wilson. It'll be delivered to your place tomorrow."

"Excellent work! I hope you didn't go to too much trouble on my account. Is that how you cut your hand?"

"Yeah, but it was no trouble at all," I said, lying, thinking it best to spare him the details. "We got a good price on it, too. You'll have to let Blocks know where you want his men to place it. It's incredibly heavy and, believe me, they'll only have one go at it. Once it's in place, you can't be changing your mind. It's a bugger to move."

"Okay. I'll settle up your invoice on that right away as well. Have arrangements been made for Sarah's funeral?"

"Yes. I asked Melanie Halliday to organize everything."

"That's the doctor's wife?" He pushed food around on his plate.

"Yes. Sarah's body was sent to Grenada for cremation. The ashes should be returned tomorrow. Melanie has chartered *OneLove* to take a small group out for a private service on Sunday." *OneLove* is a day-sail catamaran working out of Bequia. "They have a trip to the Tobago Cays that day, but Melanie was told that a half-hour funeral service at sunrise can be accommodated. Is that okay with you?"

"All very good. I couldn't have done better myself."

"By the way, Ned Watson asked if you would allow him to attend. He's the boyfriend, the one who arrived here last Saturday with Sarah. He's pretty broken up about her death." I hoped Wilson was feeling open-minded.

He sighed. "I suppose so. I have nothing personal against the guy. None of this was his fault. But I don't want Sarah's funeral to turn into a circus. Please make sure to limit the number of people. Things like this can get out of hand and attract the wrong kind."

"Okay." I hesitated before going on. "Ahhh, there are a few things I should talk over with you—other things you may not know have happened this week. You did ask me to stay out of the investigation and, believe me, I have tried. But I was already too involved, whether we like it or not."

"Yes, Geoff, I am sorry for that."

"I have to tell you, some of the stuff that has involved me is not as coincidental as has appeared. And it could be related to Sarah. So it's possible that something in what I'm about to tell you will help us discover Sarah's murderer." I paused a moment. "We found another body in your pool yesterday afternoon. It was someone who knew Sarah, a young local guy known as Big Fly."

"Yes, I know about that." Wilson looked solemn.

His answer knocked me back in my chair. How had he heard so soon after arriving?

"Who told you? The police? Your taxi driver?" If you want to know anything at all, ask a taxi driver. Al would never have said anything to Wilson on their flight from Barbados.

"I'd rather not say." Wilson looked down at his hands.

Then it struck me. Mentioning that Big Fly had been familiar to Sarah was an understatement. Their affair was the reason the

Wilsons had split. That memory was most likely the cause of the man's sudden grimness.

Embarrassed, I said, "I'm sorry, Mr. Wilson. I shouldn't have brought up the past like that."

"That's all right. It was all water under the bridge a long time ago. It's been a few years." His shaking fingers combed through a head of thick, greying hair.

After a moment, I suggested, "If it's too difficult to talk about right now, just say so. But we really do need to discuss a few things, maybe in the presence of the police. We should sort this out. It could lead to finding Sarah's murderer."

Wilson was quiet, then said, "Yes, I know. I appreciate your concern. I really do. Let's make arrangements to meet with the police in the morning and talk about everything then. Yesterday I asked you to give up your investigation because I have my reasons. I don't care to go into them at the moment, but I am intent on finding Sarah's murderer. If we talk over everything that's happened this week, we may be able to put something together. I'll contact the police in the morning. I should report in to them anyway, I suppose."

He stopped talking for a few minutes, as though lost and far away. Then he shook himself out and said, "Let's not discuss this any further tonight. I'm exhausted. I think I'll call a taxi, if it's all right with you, and get back to The Clouds. I hope you don't mind. I'm sorry Angie didn't join us. It would have been nice to see her again. She's always a sight for sore eyes." He smiled.

"That she is."

But where could she be? It was so unlike her not to call the restaurant to let me know she was going to be late. She may be an independent woman, but she's British polite and would always apologize if she couldn't make it for an appointment.

Before Wilson left, I thought I should probably play property manager for a moment and earn my keep.

"By the way, there was, ummm, quite a lot of blood in the pool yesterday, so I overdosed the water with chlorine and ran the pump for twenty-four hours to filter the water. It should be clean enough for you to use by now, but you may notice the chlorine level is still a bit high."

Wilson laughed. "That's what I like about you, Geoff! You've always treated my house like it was your own, taking good care of everything. I haven't thanked you enough for that before. I must say I've really appreciated having you here looking after the place. You've done a great job."

That made me happy—a satisfied client!

"Thanks for saying so. There's also a message I should pass on to you, but only because I promised. I don't think this is information the police necessarily need to hear tomorrow. I'm not even sure it's all that important to you either, but I promised I would tell you."

"Well, what is it?" Wilson's attention was drifting from me as he signalled the waitress for the check.

"Big Fly told me he'd tested positive for AIDS."

His eyes hadn't returned to me yet, so I could tell the full weight of this information hadn't registered. I was going to have to spell it out for him.

"He'd managed to inform Sarah before she was murdered. He asked her to tell you as well, but I don't think she had a chance to do that, did she?"

As I finished speaking, Wilson's face turned towards me, a paler shade of white, the change visible even in that dim light of the restaurant. He gulped and nodded acknowledgement. So it was definite Sarah hadn't telephoned him before she was murdered.

"Big Fly made me promise to tell you, too. In fact, he was most insistent I do so. As I've said, there's probably nothing in all of this as far as you're concerned, but Big Fly insisted I tell you to get an AIDS test, too."

"Oh, God," was all he said. Then, managing to compose himself a bit, he added, "Thanks for telling me, Geoff." He picked up the check, said, "I'll talk with you in the morning," then left to pay for dinner at the front desk.

I was a little stunned Wilson had taken the news so hard. There must have been more to the Sarah/Big Fly/Wilson relationship than even the island gossips had imagined. I sat at the table, mulling this over while finishing my glass of wine.

But the Frangi on a Thursday evening is not a place conducive to thinking, so I stood up from the table. I wanted to get home and find out what had happened to Angie. It was already close to nine o'clock. Maybe she was waiting at home, figuring our dinner wouldn't last as long as it had.

I left the restaurant enclosure to make my way through the growing crowd of people hanging around listening to the steel band. Then I saw Mike, beer bottle in hand, strolling towards me from the dinghy dock.

"Hey, mate, what happened to your . . . "

"Don't ask."

"Okay, but I'm glad I found you. I want to confirm something I just heard from the boys sitting on the dock. Did Sarah still have a key to Wilson's house?"

"No, not as far as I know. I have the only key on the island. Wilson, of course, has his own. He told me he changed the locks after the divorce. Why?"

"Well, the word is that someone else has a key and is using Wilson's house for more than just a place to store murder victims. I don't know exactly what's going on. I'll hang out here for awhile longer to see if I can scare up anything else on this key business, or what might be happening at Wilson's. If we can find the person with the key, then we'll also find the murderer. That's my theory. In the meantime," he added, grabbing my upper arm and squeezing, "watch your back, mate. People say something big is going down on Bequia. I have a suspicion you might be considered a spoiler in the proceedings."

I looked down at his hand still on my arm, pursed my lips, and said, "Thanks for the warning, man. And for the new information. Wilson and I are meeting with the police in the morning. I'll raise this idea with him then. I have to go."

He released his grip and turned away. I watched him walk towards the bar to continue his covert operations, armed only with a beer. Tough life. I headed back towards the beach.

Leaving the Frangi, I walked along the paved walkway border-ing the sea towards where I'd parked. As I got close to my car, I saw the Brethren standing beside it, looking anxious rather than their usual out-and-out-wasted.

Before I could say anything, Rasta Bongo motioned for me to hurry, and when I came up next to them, he surveyed all around, making sure we wouldn't be overheard.

"We finds something," he said in a whisper.

Not again! I smacked my forehead with my good hand, but hit the bruise over my eye.

"Owww! Okay, what did you find this time, guys? The cutlass that killed Big Fly?"

"No, not dat," said Rasta I-Toe, not understanding my sarcasm, or seeming to notice my injuries. "We no finds de cutlass. We finds money. And, Geoff, it be plenty, plenty money."

"Where did you find that?" I asked, suddenly serious. By the looks on their faces, it must have been a lot.

"We chook up de rest of de bush by Wilson's," Rasta Bongo an-swered. "We finds more things bury there in de garden. We finds two suitcase fill with money. American money. Plenty American money." They both nodded at me.

I was taken aback. Suitcases of money? Now what was going on? Everything was being blown way out of proportion.

"I hope you left those suitcases where you found them. Who knows who's involved in all of this, or what they might do if that money's not there when they go back for it?"

"We carries de suitcase home," Rasta I-Toe said. "All dat money bury, there be something wrong with dat, we thinks, so we carries dem home. We no touch de money, Geoff. We good man; we no t'ief it."

I knew these guys were too honest to pocket even one of those bills, as tempted as they should have been by the sight of so much cash. From what they'd said, it was probably more than they could ever hope to earn in their combined lifetimes.

"I trust you both implicitly, guys. But you shouldn't have moved the suitcases. Just like with the gun and clothes yesterday, whoever buried the suitcases may go back to look for them. Come on, jump in the car. I'll drive you back to your place. We'll pick up the suitcases and return them to The Clouds. It might be tricky burying them tonight. Wilson arrived today. We just finished dinner. Let's hope he was as tired as he looked and has already gone to bed."

The three of us were climbing into the car when someone along the waterfront shouted, "FIRE!" Then other voices joined in and people near us began pointing. I searched across the Harbour and saw a definite glow in the sky from down by the end of the shore at Hamilton. Then suddenly there was an explosion of flames, followed by *Ka-Boom!* People on the walkway screamed.

I shouted at the Brethren, "Get into the car! Fast! That looks like it's down by my place!" They pulled their legs in and slammed the doors.

Trying to keep my eyes on the road, I drove out of the parking lot and sped through town. The Brethren kept watching the fire and gasped a split second before we all heard a second explosion. Then they said they lost sight of the fire altogether as we moved through the centre of town. I increased speed and prayed the one island fire truck wasn't out by the airport, all the way at the other end of Bequia. As we approached the far side of Hamilton, I could see the fire was on Henry's property, although not by the boathouse, as I'd feared. One whole side of his villa was completely engulfed in flames.

We jumped out of the car and the Brethren joined the crowd of neighbours that had been gathering to watch. Someone came over to tell me they'd already called the police. I ran down the hill to the boathouse, yelling, "Angie, Angie!" for all my life was worth. The door to the house was still locked. I jiggled the key in and turned the handle, but had a gut feeling once I'd opened the door that Angie wasn't there and hadn't been in the house since I'd closed up earlier. I called out for Gus, but figured he'd deserted the scene at the first whiff of smoke. I couldn't decide if that made him smart or a wimp. Hauling out a length of hose, I called the Brethren over to help. Any effort to put out a fire of that size would take more water than a garden-variety hose could deliver, but I had to do something while we waited for the fire truck. I couldn't stand there watching and not try to be useful in some way. Then I heard the distant *pam-pom, pam-pom* wailing of the siren from across the bay.

In the meantime, we stretched out the hose to its length and began spraying at the fire. The next thing I knew, Mike was by my side, helping.

"God, Mike! Do you believe this?"

He grabbed my shoulder and shouted into my face. "I saw it from over at the Frangi. Came in the dinghy as fast as I could. Brought a couple of the boys with me."

Neighbours had begun organizing a bucket brigade, so Mike went over to give them a hand.

Our combined efforts weren't making a noticeable difference—we were just putting ourselves in more danger. The fire truck arrived and the crew was able to control and contain the fire in a short while, although it still seemed to take a lifetime. The police arrived at the same time that the fire was extinguished.

When we could see the extent of the damage, it looked bad from a distance. One whole wing of the house, the area furthest from the boathouse, had been destroyed.

"I want a word with you, Geoff," the inspector said.

I didn't reply, just turned away; I was leading him down to the boathouse when Rasta Bongo ran towards us, breathless.

"Geoff, Geoff, come, come!" he said, shouting, then turned to run ahead along the path between the villa and the boathouse, taking us close to a thicket. He stopped and pointed at the ground. "There!"

Angie was lying on her back beside the path but tucked away under the bushes, out of direct sight. It was so dark, and I'd been too focused on the fire. I hadn't seen her there earlier when I'd first run to the boathouse. Gus lay beside her.

"Somebody call the doctor," I screamed, falling down on my knees by her side. I put my face next to her mouth and felt a faint wisp of air lick at my cheek. She was unconscious but still breathing. She was still breathing!

"Oh, Angie, my beautiful Ange. I'm so sorry," I said, whispering, unaccustomed tears beginning to course down my face.

I wanted to hug her, to shield her from any more harm, but it was already too late. She was burned, and in a bad state, so I was afraid to touch her at all.

Chapter Eight

The next morning, I sat in the boathouse, slumped at the kitchen table, elbows on the surface, head propped up in my hands, unable to stop reliving the previous night's horror.

"Mr. Geoff, I makes you some coffee," said Celesta. "You must eat. It good for you. Miss Angie will wants you to eats."

The Brethren had taken over when my life fell apart a few hours before. They were the ones who called in the housekeepers, Celesta and Lucella, to look after me while Doc and Melanie tended to Angie. They also offered to oversee my business until I could resume control. Rasta Bongo and Lucella had already left to work at one of the houses, leaving Celesta at the boathouse to mother me. All my employees were pitching in. I was grateful I'd hired good people—people I could count on in a time of crisis.

Some of my neighbours had also dropped by early that morning to offer assistance. Mrs. Gregg delivered a batch of cookies she'd baked during the night, saying, "Geoff, I hopes these helps in some way."

"Thank you, Mrs. Gregg. That's so kind."

"I worry about Angie. How she is?"

"Angie went to Barbados. I haven't heard from Dr. Halliday yet, but he and Melanie are taking care of her."

"I prays for she. You tells she from me, from all de neighbours, we hopes she be back soon. When you goes to she, you comes by me first, takes some of de flowers from my garden. I know she like dat." Mrs. Gregg smiled with a broad mouth and stretched out her arms for a hug. I leaned over and allowed the short woman to smother me with concern. I was comforted knowing I was surrounded by friends.

After Mrs. Gregg left, Celesta insisted again, "Mr. Geoff, you eats." There was no resisting. Celesta had single-handedly raised five children with a strict and religious demeanour, so she was not a woman to cross. Plus, she outweighs me by about a hundred and fifty pounds. So I drank the coffee she'd made and tried to eat some of the food she'd prepared, just to keep her happy. I even managed to nibble at one of Mrs. Gregg's cookies.

It had been a long and exhausting night.

Doc responded at once to my cry for help.

"I'm right here, Geoff. Let me have a look." He moved me off to the side from where I was kneeling while Melanie helped me to my feet.

"We saw the fire from our house," she said. "Dave called the ambulance. It should have been here by now."

Soon after, the ambulance did arrive, and, less than twenty minutes since Rasta Bongo had found her, Angie was finally being transported to the clinic, accompanied by Doc and Melanie. Although she's not a trained nurse, we all knew Mel would be a great help attending to Angie.

"Geoff," Rasta I-Toe said, catching me by surprise as I watched the ambulance pull away. "What we does wit de dog? He gots burned feets."

"Oh, ah, right." I looked over at Gus, who must have regained consciousness while we were getting Angie into the ambulance. Rasta Bongo was crouched by the dog's side, maintaining control over him, although Gus didn't seem interested in going anywhere at all. Most of his hair had been singed and he was a sorry sight, not unlike the way he looked when he first adopted us.

"I guess he'll have to go to the vet in Kingstown tomorrow. Can you and Bongo handle that?"

"Yes," he said. He snapped around in a turn and joined Rasta Bongo.

Mike assisted me in further dealings with the police.

"Inspector, maybe you should start questioning the neighbours." Mike waved a hand around at the crowd as it began to disperse.

"That is a good suggestion," Kydd said. In an unusually loud voice, with one hand cupped by the side of his mouth, he shouted, "Everyone remain where you are. I will speak with all of you."

Some grumbled and kept walking. Others, older women for the most part, shuffled their feet to form a closer grouping around Kydd. His work would be cut out for him.

Mike said, "C'mon, mate. We'll take Doc's wheels. He left me the keys."

We began walking towards the car, but Kydd reached out to grab me.

"You must stay here where I can watch you. I have some more questions."

"What?" I lost it altogether and started screaming. "My girl-friend has come close to dying! We don't know yet if she'll recover. Of course I'm going to go!"

"I cannot take de chance you might use de opportunity to leave de country."

"Oh, for Christ's sake!"

"Inspector," Mike said, moving in between the two of us. "Why don't you send one of your corporals with Geoff, if you don't trust him."

The inspector thought for a moment. "Hmm, that is a good idea. All right, you may go."

I shook his hand off my arm.

"But you must check with me again in de morning." He turned to one of his corporals and pointed. "You, go."

I didn't even stop to thank him, just ran to the car with Mike, escorted by the corporal, my baby-sitter.

When we first arrived at the clinic, Angie was still unconscious. Doc, Melanie, and the night nurse did what they could with her burns, which were first and second degree. They put her on oxygen and an IV drip as well, but Doc admitted, "There's only so much I can do for Angie here. I have to get her to Barbados as soon as possible. The hospital facilities are better there, certainly superior to what's available on St. Vincent. Since we have to wait until daylight to move her by plane to either place, anyway, I'd rather send her to Barbados."

"Whatever needs to be done to make Angie well again, I'll agree to it. Do whatever you consider best," I said, holding back tears.

The Bequia Airport is not sanctioned to allow planes to take off or land at night. The claim had been that the runway lights needed repairing, but that work has been completed, so my guess is now they simply can't convince the airport staff to stay on the job outside regular hours. Not having access to twenty-four hour emergency air evacuation is certainly a detriment to the island. And it's a problem that's being addressed on a regular basis, especially by the expatriate community, but to no avail. Complaints always fall on deaf government ears.

We had a long wait until daylight. It was still only 11:30 p.m.

"I'll phone Al and make the arrangements for his plane so we can get Angie out of here first thing," Mike said.

"Thanks, man."

He left the clinic. Then I turned to Doc and asked, "What do you think?" I nodded towards Angie. "Honest opinion."

"Most of the burns are first degree, so she's not as bad as you imagine. But there must have been more smoke than fire wherever she got caught. It was likely smoke inhalation that knocked her unconscious, and that could cause the greatest problems in the long run. She must remain on oxygen for awhile to help her breathe. She should be stable by morning, though. Stable enough to safely make the flight to Barbados. I'll go along with her and so will Melanie. Even though Mel's not a nurse, being a friend will go a longer way to keeping Angie calm."

"Thanks, Doc. Thanks to both of you."

I knew it was out of the question I would ever be allowed to make the trip with Angie. Still under orders not to leave the country, I was stuck on Bequia, but assured she'd be in good hands—the best hands, in fact. Besides, I'd just be in the way with all my worrying.

"But after you get Angie to Barbados, what do you think will happen? How bad is she?"

"Once she regains consciousness, I'll have a better idea of the extent of her injuries, but don't worry—we'll look after her. And she'll get excellent care on Barbados; I'll make sure of that. I'll call ahead before we leave and make the necessary arrangements with the hospital. I have a colleague, a friend, over there. I'll alert him about Angie's situation. Everyone will be ready for us."

We all remained quiet and, a few minutes later, Angie began to come around. It was an unbelievable relief to see her eyes opening once again. I was already standing by her side so while she was waking up I bent down to get as close to her as I could without touching her body. She reached up to my face with one bandaged hand, placed it on my cheek, and groped for my hand with her other. Doc removed the oxygen mask. Then, gathering her strength, Angie made an attempt to speak, but all that came out of her mouth was a series of croaks that sounded more like the *quark-quark* of a mangrove cuckoo.

"Don't try to speak now, Angie," Doc said. "I don't want you aggravating any damage that may have been done by the smoke to your throat and lungs."

But there was no stopping her. She had something to say and was determined to get it out, so she pulled my head down until my ear was by her mouth. Struggling with her voice, she became frustrated at my not being able to understand, but on the third attempt, I heard something in her whisper that began to make sense. I lifted my head away from her face to look at her, reading her eyes. She gave me a slight nod then reached up and pulled my head back down to her mouth and whispered a little louder and clearer this time. I stood up, looked at her again, and she gave me another encouraging nod, gesturing with her bandaged hand that I repeat what she had said.

"Hermut," I announced to the room. "Angie said Hermut did this to her."

Angie nodded again, this time in agreement, and squeezed her eyes shut. A tear began rolling down one cheek. She continued holding my hand, but her grip had relaxed.

"That bastard!" I said, my other hand reaching up to cover my now blue-black eye.

"You mean, Hermut who owns Bob's Beach Bar?" Melanie said with a gasp, as astonished by the news as her husband appeared to be.

Again, Angie simply nodded in response.

"Corporal." I turned to my baby-sitter, my voice waking him from the short doze he'd been indulging in while leaning against the wall, ignoring our drama. "Please go to the police station immediately and tell the inspector I think we know who started the fire. Please ask him to come to the clinic straight away."

The corporal shook himself awake and left.

The police station is right behind the clinic, so it should not have taken long for the inspector to join us. However, when he didn't show up at all, we assumed it was because he'd received the information from the corporal and was out searching for Hermut.

"I saw Hermut on the boat when I went to Kingstown this morning," I said to Angie, Doc, and Mel. Pointing at my eye, I said, "That's who did this to me. I don't know which ferry he took back from St. Vincent, but I don't think he was on the same boat as me this afternoon." Leaning back down close to Angie, I continued. "I can't, for the life of me, figure out what would have made him do this to you; maybe he was just trying to get back at me for what happened on the ferry."

She reached out to my eye, outlining the surrounding unnatural colours with a finger.

"But, whatever the reason, I want him caught and punished. Brutally punished!"

Angie placed a finger on my lips, shushing me.

I was anxious to hear more details that night from Angie, to clear up what had happened, but instead said, "Sorry, Ange. I should probably keep quiet now and let the inspector question you when he gets here. My anger isn't helping, is it?"

But Doc was insistent, anyway. "I don't want Angie straining her voice by making a report tonight."

Until Angie could talk, we wouldn't know the details. It was enough for us now to have the name of who had been involved in starting the fire and injuring Angie. With that information, the police could make an arrest and we'd be well on our way to sorting everything out—that is, presuming Hermut was also involved in the other things that had happened to us that week.

We all remained quiet after Angie's disclosure, allowing her to rest. Doc had given her something to alleviate the pain, and offered me the same as well, but I wanted to remain lucid, so only accepted a couple of Aspirin. I continued holding Angie's hand, giving it a reassuring squeeze every once in a while, just to let her know I was still there.

Mike came back some time later to tell us everything was organized. "Al says he'll meet you at the airport at five. That way, he should be ready to take off at first light. To his credit, too, he actually managed to impress upon the airport staff that this is indeed an emergency and he *will* fly out of Bequia as soon as possible. It's a miracle he was not only able to track down all the necessary employees but also convince them to take his request seriously and promise they'd get out of bed in time."

"And lucky for us Carnival is over and that neither World Cup football nor a West Indies cricket test match are being played," Doc added.

During any of these events, it's almost impossible to get Vincentians to work their regular paid hours, let alone come in for overtime.

"I'll drive home to pack a change of clothes and get our passports, Dave," Melanie said.

"Good plan. Why don't you go directly to the airport from home and meet us at five."

"If you need Angie's passport, maybe you could pick that up from our place, as well," I said, offering my keys.

"We won't worry about Angie's passport," Doc said. I'm sure my Barbados colleague can handle the technicalities if anyone decides to become officious."

Melanie left.

Doc studied my face. "You should go home now. You look beat. There's nothing more you can do here, anyway."

"I can hold Angie's hand." I felt a tighter squeeze from her in response. "I'll wait until you're ready to go."

"Would you like me to have a look at your eye?"

"Thanks, but my hand is probably in more need of medical attention." I raised it to show him. "That's another long story, best left for cocktail hour."

Doc unwrapped my home-style, one-handed bandaging job, cleaned out the cut, and rewrapped it in fresh gauze.

Then Doc and Mike sat in a couple of chairs so they could nap and I remained next to Angie's bed. She'd closed her eyes; the medication must have helped her relax because she appeared to be sleeping. Praying might have helped then, if only to pass the hours while we waited. I spent the entire time staring at my beautiful Angie, willing her, and our lives, to return to normal.

The time to leave finally arrived. Doc assured me, "I'll call from Barbados and give you a full report on Angie's condition as soon as I can. But, Geoff, as your doctor, I prescribe that you go home and get into bed. You need some sleep. She'll be fine, don't worry."

I continued holding Angie's hand until the moment she was placed in the ambulance, then waved goodbye and waited as they drove away.

Mike walked back with me to the boathouse. He'd left his dinghy tied to my dock.

"Man, we really don't realize how precious something is until we almost lose it," I said.

"True." We remained silent the rest of the way.

There was neither vehicle nor person on the road at that time of the morning. The tree frogs were still chirping, and a few birds were beginning to sing as first light broke over the hills surrounding the Harbour. Other than several fishermen already out in their boats in the Bay, roosters crowing, and assorted stray dogs running around town barking at one another, the rest of Bequia was still asleep, and oblivious.

The Brethren had made a protective bed for Gus out of a cardboard box and some towels from the bathroom. They were busy tending to him as Mike and I walked into the house. When they began working for me, I had given the Brethren a basic first aid course. They were putting that knowledge to work and had bandaged up Gus as best they could.

"Geoff, I and I takes Gus over on de first ferry. I takes he to de animal doctor." Rasta I-Toe's offer touched me. He was just as concerned for my dog as I was for Angie. We called a taxi.

Celesta and Lucella had arrived at my house in the meantime, and the women were already bustling around, tidying up the boathouse.

Mike said, "I'm off, mate. Looks like you're set." There were enough people taking care of me that one more would cause everyone to trip. He added, "I'll contact you later in the morning and find out if there's any new information about Angie." He walked to the end of the dock, got into the dinghy, and motored back to his boat.

I gave Rasta I-Toe some money for the taxi, boat fare, breakfast on board, and the initial vet bills and, as soon as the taxi arrived, Rasta I-Toe carried Gus in the box, set both in the back of the canopied truck, and sat down on one of the benches next to the dog for the drive into town to catch the first boat. Rasta Bongo and Lucella went with them. "We goes to de Englishman," Rasta Bongo said, their plan being to continue on after dropping off Rasta I-Toe and Gus at the ferry wharf. They would be able to get an early start on the weekly work at another house I manage out in Spring. "Then we comes back to de boathouse soon. We helps Celesta looks after you, Geoff." Together, we could all begin the arduous task of sifting through the damage up at the villa.

After I finished as much breakfast as I could stomach, and Celesta was satisfied with my attempt, I thought I should start making some phone calls. In hindsight, it would have been smart had I contacted the police before anyone else, but my slight nasty streak directed me to first inform Henry of his recent loss. I hoped it would be a big blow to him. He deserved that much for being so slow to pay me what was my due. I knew I'd be able to reach him at home at that time of the morning.

When he answered the phone, I said, "Henry, I'm glad I caught you. I've got news, and it isn't good. Angie was badly burned in a fire at your villa last night. I don't know the full extent of the damage yet, but it looks like one whole wing has been destroyed."

Henry surprised me. "I'm really sorry to hear about Angie. Give her my love and tell her I hope she has a speedy recovery."

So Henry was human after all. I thanked him for his concern. Then he surprised me again.

"As for my house, maybe it's time I sold. I hear new offshore banking regulations are being put into place there as well as in other Caribbean countries. It's going to make it more difficult for people like me to hold accounts, so I was thinking of moving my money soon, anyway. Apparently Belize is promoting itself as the new tax haven. It might be a good financial move in the long run if I were to get out of St. Vincent and the Grenadines altogether, right now. What do you think?"

Impatient with him, I said, "I can't help you with decisions about moving money. If you really want advice, you'd better discuss that with the legion of lawyers and financial advisors you keep on retainer."

"Would you be interested in buying the property from me? The villa and the boathouse? I know the villa isn't worth as much now, from what you've told me of the fire damage, but you and Angie already live in the boathouse. All in all, it would be a good investment for you, buddy, and you wouldn't have to move out either. Once that villa's rebuilt, and the insurance coverage I have should pay for that, it'll bring in a tidy little rental income again. And don't worry, I'll sell you the place at a good price. What do you think, buddy?" He sounded pleased with this sudden idea.

I couldn't believe his absolute audacity in making such a suggestion, so I didn't hesitate one moment, returning with, "I have an even better idea, *buddy*. How about if you *give* me the property, both houses, free and clear, in exchange for what you and the boys still owe me on that other little deal? That sounds fair to me. And while you're at it, you could also throw in whatever it will cost to rebuild the villa, over and above whatever insurance settlement you receive." I didn't stop the anger from entering my voice, wanting Henry to know just how pissed off I'd become with my former business partners for having jerked me around those past two years. I'd lost my patience.

With a nervous laugh, Henry replied, "Well, I don't know about this. I'll have to run the idea past the other guys first, but your proposal certainly does have some merit."

This would be a cheaper way out for the boys—paying me off with Henry's property rather than having to cough up what they really owed.

Warming up to the suggestion, Henry said, "I'm not sure the boys will agree to pay for rebuilding the villa as well, but if we do transfer over the land, it would have to be with the stipulation that you have no further claims on us. There'd be no coming back for more money at a later date."

I knew now I had the upper hand. "Henry, I can absolutely promise that you and the boys will never hear another word from me again, ever! And I can guarantee the pleasure will most definitely be all mine!"

I was relieved this situation was being settled, after all this time.

"I'm even willing to make that promise in writing, if you want." That last offer was quite generous of me, although I knew full well the guys would never be happy with a paper trail leading anyone to the truth about our fraudulent deeds.

"No, no, Bob. A gentleman's agreement will be fine."

Without question, it was worth my peace of mind to know this whole crooked deal with them would be over and finished, for once and for all, and would no longer haunt me. I had been the only one to voice my reluctance in the beginning, when we began organizing the scam in the first place, yet I had suffered the most.

"Frankly, I'll be happy to sever my ties with the bunch of you. So much for old friends."

"Fine." Henry stated, now sounding strictly business-like. "When I see the guys at the office this morning, I'll run past them what you and I discussed and, if they agree, we'll have the lawyer look after transferring the deed to the property right away."

"Good. The sooner the better. But one other thing, Henry: I want the property transferred to Angie's name, not mine. Your lawyer can contact me when he's ready with the paperwork. Give my love to the guys when you see them, Henry. Tell them it's been a real slice knowing all of you." I laughed and slammed down the phone.

And I bid a final bye-bye to my former-self Bob while I was at it.

I had been so angry with Henry that I hadn't thought to tell him we had a good idea of who burned down his place. But he wouldn't have known Hermut, anyway. Come to think of it—Henry hadn't shown the least bit of interest at all in the fire itself, only in selling the damaged house . . .

Even though I was steeping in anger after dealing with Henry, that call took a huge load off my mind. I'd finally come to the realization that my oldest and dearest friends really didn't care about me at all. Out of sight, out of mind, I guess. In this case, absence had not made the heart grow fonder. I'd trusted them to look after my best interests and they'd let me down, big time. This sudden discovery was a huge disappointment, knowing now I could no longer rely on their friendship, but it was a relief at the same time to understand where I stood with people I'd once considered my best friends, relief that this longstanding, one-sided relationship with them was finally over. With friends like that, who needs to worry about enemies.

Trying to dismiss them from my mind, I looked over at the clock. It was seven so I thought I'd better phone the police and find out if their search for Hermut had been fruitful. The inspector could have been trying to call while I was wasting all that time on the phone with Henry.

After the corporal on dispatch at the station put me through to the inspector, I said, "Any luck yet, Inspector?"

"Any luck with what?" His voice sounded puzzled.

"Finding Hermut Landecker, of course." I was just as puzzled he didn't seem to know what I was talking about. "Angie woke up and was able to tell me Hermut's name. He started the fire. I sent the corporal back to the station to tell you straight away so you could begin your search and bring him in."

"But I was not at de station last night," he said. "I was, ah, un-avoidably detained elsewhere. I did not receive your message." He sounded embarrassed. As well he should have been. My first thought was that he had spent the rest of the night after the fire with his girl-friend, or some other place he shouldn't have been, leaving orders at the station that he was not to be disturbed. I didn't ask why he hadn't been available, and I honestly didn't care enough anymore to want to hear his excuse. My only concern at that moment was we'd lost precious time and were getting nowhere fast.

"Well, could you please send someone out *now* to look for Lan-decker?" I said, not able to control my temper. "Until we get more information from Angie, we won't know exactly what happened at the villa. She's not able to talk at all, under her doctor's orders, but can't you use what she said and at least bring the man in for ques-tioning? I have an idea Hermut may have been behind more than just the fire and could possibly tell us something else. Please find him and question him."

"I am sorry for this, Geoff. I will go out right now to look for de man."

If I didn't find the guy first. I was ready to search for him my-self, and rip out his heart with my bare hands for what he'd done to Ange.

In fact, I began formulating a plan to do just that.

"But two other things, Inspector. Mr. Wilson and I would like to meet with you this morning, at ten o'clock, if that's convenient. We both thought it would do a lot more good to talk everything over in your presence."

"Yes, Geoff. I will return to de station then."

"And, the other thing is, before the fire began, the Brethren told me they'd dug up two suitcases filled with US cash."

"Who found them?"

"The two guys who work for me. The Rastas."

"Rastas!" He spat out the word. "Are you sure they are trustworthy?"

The good Methodist inspector's prejudicial petticoat was showing.

"Yes, well, don't worry. We have the suitcases secured. I'll turn them over to you as soon as possible."

"Please do so. It is probably contraband."

Oh, do you think? This guy was more like Inspector Clouseau than Inspector Morse. I said goodbye and hung up the phone as fast as I could.

Celesta swept over to me from the kitchen at a speed that belied her large frame.

"Mr. Geoff, I hears you on de telephone. You says Hermut do dat to Miss Angie last night?"

"Yeah," I said, starting to stand. "I'm going out to look for the bastard!" Celesta grabbed my arm. "Oh, sorry, I didn't mean to use language like that."

"Why— he some bad man, Mr. Geoff. He plenty bad. Everybody know dat. People say he do plenty bad things. You calls him whatever you wants, he deserve dat."

I'd forgotten to tell my staff about Angie pointing the finger at Hermut. I'd assumed none of them would have known anything about him, anyway, other than that he was a restaurateur and a foreigner.

"What kind of bad things, Celesta?"

"I no know, only dat dey plenty bad and he be a mean man."

"What he did to Angie last night was certainly in character, then."

"But you must stay. De police finds him now. You waits to hear from de doctor." Celesta patted me on the shoulder and went back to cleaning.

I phoned Wilson to fill him in on everything that had happened, including Angie's accusation of Hermut. On his side of the island, he would not yet have known of the commotion after he left the Frangi. The Clouds is pretty well cut off from everything on the Harbour side. He wouldn't even have seen the flames or heard the sirens. Besides, I had to call anyway to let him know of the arrangement I'd made for us to meet with the inspector. Once I did reach him, Wilson's reaction to my news was more than the expected one of simple surprise.

When I explained about the fire and said, "Angie identified Hermut," Wilson gasped.

Then he said in a low voice, "Geoff, you should know, right now, that Hermut spent the night here at The Clouds, but he'd left by the time I got up this morning. I do want to talk with you and the police about all of this, immediately, but I think it prudent I contact my lawyer in St. Vincent first and try to get him over on the next boat to sit with me for our meeting. I would like legal counsel on all this before I proceed." Then he made an attempt to assure me. "You'll have to take my word for this, though; I knew nothing of the fire, or of anything else Hermut may have been involved in this past week, or at any other time, for that matter. He's a friend, and has been for a long time, but he's an extremely private man, as you may know. I really had no idea he was capable of doing what you say he did to Angie, if what she's accusing him of is true."

"Oh, it's the truth all right. My Angie doesn't lie, and certainly not about something like this. But I believe you weren't involved. I'll wait for your lawyer to arrive. The inspector is supposed to be out right now searching for Hermut. I'm hoping the police will find him before too long, so we can get down to the bottom of things. Until then, it's probably best if we don't speak further about any of this."

Wilson was now our only connection with Hermut, and he was also the link between the fire and Sarah's murder. If he came in to talk to the police, willingly, to tell us what he knew, even though accompanied by his lawyer, we might be able to pin everything on Hermut and find out why he had done the things he had that past week.

"Thanks. I'll call the police as soon as I've contacted my lawyer. I'll insist he catch the next ferry and we'll meet shortly after that— say around ten-thirty rather than ten o'clock? And, Geoff, I'm grateful you believe me, believe that I had no part in this. I am truly sorry Angie was hurt. I'd like to pay for any medical expenses you incur."

"For Angie's sake, thanks, Mr. Wilson. I'll see you later."

I knew that, by the time we were to meet, the police would have rounded up Hermut. Then we could discover the truth and put an end to that past week.

I showered, changed, popped a slice of now-cold bacon into my mouth, and drank some more of Celesta's fresh-brewed coffee. This time I drank without coercion.

Doc finally called before eight. "Angie will be fine, but she's going to have to stay in the Barbados hospital for a few days. The doctors still don't want her talking at all. I'm going to fly back to Bequia with Al in about half an hour. Mel has offered to stay for the rest of the day and keep Angie company. She'll catch a ride back later this afternoon. Al has to return then to pick up some charter passengers."

It was a great relief knowing our friends—our genuine friends—were looking after both of us.

Not wanting to detain Doc and Al any longer, I said, "I'll catch up with you later. I have a lot to tell you. Please give Angie my love."

"I anticipated and already did that." Doc laughed. "See you soon."

After hanging up the phone, Celesta and I took a walk up the hill together to survey the damage at the villa. Along the way, Celesta said, "You knows my boy, Dagbert? He a policeman now."

"Really? I didn't know that."

"Sure you does. Miss Angie, she know. I tells she so when he graduate."

"Sorry, I guess that information didn't filter down to me. My congratulations. You must be very proud."

"Yes, please!" Celesta nodded, beaming as though her face were about to split. "I plenty proud! He a constable and station on Bequia. He say he be there, at de pool, after you finds de white woman body Monday."

I thought for a moment and remembered the rather eager young constable. "That was Dagbert? I wouldn't have known. What a thing for him to deal with on a new job."

"Yes, but he be a good policeman. I makes sure of dat!" She waved her hand about in a threatening manner.

"I know you will." I wondered if any other St. Vincent police would receive a lickin' from their mothers if they didn't perform well. Maybe that's just what the Royal St. Vincent and the Grenadines Police Force needed.

We arrived at what had been the entrance to the villa. The fire must have started in the kitchen and the one wing containing that room was destroyed. The house was built as two separate sections connected by a central courtyard. The other wing, containing the bedrooms and a living area, was still closed up so the flames had not touched it, although smoke damage to the outside of that building was extensive.

I knew Henry owned a comprehensive stash of videotapes, mostly porn, and he kept them hidden in a small, locked room beside the kitchen. That room and all its contents were burned to the ground. I figured it had been the burning videos that caused such a large amount of smoke.

"Mr. Geoff, comes here," Celesta said, pointing at the remains of two one hundred-pound propane tanks Henry insisted keeping on hand to provide fuel for the kitchen stove and barbeque. They must have been what exploded, the two explosions we witnessed from the Harbour.

"The whole place is certainly a mess," I said. "There's nothing left of the kitchen, but this wing can be rebuilt. The other will probably need a good paint job."

Celesta nodded in agreement. I left her at the villa to start opening up the windows and doors in the undamaged section to air out the bedrooms. I walked back down to the boathouse.

It was lonely for me around the place without Gus literally dogging my every step—even lonelier without Angie. I tried not to think about it.

By then, it was close to ten o'clock and the ferry was motoring around the headland, entering the Harbour. I got into my car and drove to the wharf to see if Wilson's lawyer was among the arriving passengers.

Chapter Nine

Wilson was standing on the wharf, waiting for the ferry. I decided not to approach, giving him a chance to meet with his lawyer alone first before they went to the police station. Rasta I-Toe was on the upper deck of the ferry, in the lineup with the other passengers coming down the companionway. He saw me and waved. I ambled over to talk with him when he stepped off the lowered loading ramp.

"Geoff, no probs. Gus be okay," he said. "De doctor, he say he keep Gus a few days. He say he calls you later."

"Thanks, Ras. Thanks for looking after Gus. I really appreciate everything all of you have done for us. And I know Angie will be happy to hear Gus is going to be okay."

"No probs, man."

"About the money you and Bongo found—I have half a mind to tell you to keep it, but I already mentioned it to the inspector. I don't want you to take it to the police just yet, though. Please make sure it's secure for now. I'll drive to your place later and pick it up."

"Okay, Geoff. Nobody ever come by to t'ieve from a Rasta house. Dey all thinks we gots nothing. Nobody think we might gots some money. We tells nobody, only you. It be safe by us."

"That's true. Oh, and I forgot to mention earlier—Angie identified Hermut as the one who started the fire."

Rasta I-Toe went wide-eyed.

"But dat man on de boat dis morning," he said. "I see'd him. He walk on behind I and I. He goes to Town." Locals refer to Kingstown as Town, usually Big Town to differentiate it from Port Elizabeth, which is known as Little Town.

"He went back there again this morning? Hermut was on the boat when I went to St. Vincent yesterday. But there should have been a policeman on the wharf when the boat left. Do you remember?"

There's always supposed to be a policeman stationed at the wharf, whenever ferryboats arrive and depart, to watch for undesirables getting on and off the boats.

"Yeah, there be a police," Rasta I-Toe answered.

It was likely that word about Hermut hadn't gotten around yet to all the police by 6:30 a.m. After all, the inspector hadn't known to search for him until I'd mentioned to do so on the phone, and that was well after the first boat had left the wharf, but I assumed someone in the lower ranks would have taken the initiative to begin working on Angie's information. I guess I was wrong.

"I'm on my way to the station now. I'll tell the inspector to call the police on St. Vincent and get them to start searching for Hermut on the mainland right away."

Rasta Bongo and Lucella drove past in a taxi. Rasta I-Toe whistled to stop them and turned back to me. "I sees you, Geoff. We all goes back to de house." He ran over to hitch a ride. I watched him climb into the back of the taxi and begin, accompanied by exaggerated arm gestures, to fill them in on the news as they drove away.

After they left, Blocks passed by on his way through town. His truck's bed was loaded with about eight workers, all standing, and Wilson's copper. They were on their way out to The Clouds. I waved Blocks down to give him directions. "Hi, Blocks. You know how to get up to the house?" He nodded. "Wilson isn't there. I just saw him on the wharf."

"Where you wants de copper?"

"If they can manage it, have the guys carry it down the path to the right of the house. There's a cleared area in the garden."

"All right. I checks. Sees you later, Geoff." He drove off, and the entire crew waved at me as the truck rounded the corner. They were jostled by the turn, but not enough to cause anyone to lose footing.

I hoofed it the rest of the way up the road to the police station.

Everyone else was already assembled in the station's reception area by the time I arrived.

"Inspector, may I have a word with you first," I said, motioning him over to the side. "I've been told Hermut went to St. Vincent on the six-thirty ferry."

He looked at me and, without a word, turned and walked into his office. I heard him dialling, then he said, "I must speak with de commissioner. This is urgent!"

While we waited for the inspector to return, Wilson introduced me to his lawyer.

"Geoff, this is Mr. Williams."

This was getting confusing: Wilson, Watson, Williams. And to make things worse, there are a number of other lawyers with the surname Williams who practice in St. Vincent. I didn't recognize this particular man, who was elderly and looked trustworthy. I hoped, for Wilson's sake, he was one of the minute number of honest lawyers practicing in the country.

"Should we go into the room and sit down?" Wilson asked. He held out a hand and ushered Williams, me, and a corporal into an adjoining meeting room.

We sat on opposite sides of a long table, the corporal at one end. He produced a clean pad of paper and two pens. I told Wilson the news I'd given the inspector. He exchanged a glance with his lawyer, then stared at the tabletop, but said nothing. The inspector joined us a few minutes later.

"I have asked headquarters to search for Mr. Landecker on the mainland," he said as he slipped into the last vacant chair. He pointed at the corporal and added, "Our meeting will be recorded." The corporal sat erect, hand holding a pen poised over the paper.

Wilson looked ashen. He began by saying, "First of all, I want you to know I had no idea Hermut was involved in last night's fire, or in anything else, for that matter. He spent the night at my house, but he was gone by the time I woke up. I now realize he went to St. Vincent this morning. He didn't tell me any of his plans and I don't know where he might have gone. He arrived at my house last night shortly after I had dinner with you, Geoff," he said, turning to me. "Hermut is a quiet man, generally, and when we're together, we usually don't talk much about, ah, anything at all. In fact, the most agitated and animated I've ever seen him was when I arrived at the house yesterday afternoon. He was waiting for me when I drove in from the airport, but he left before the taxi came back to take me to the Frangi. I don't know what happened to upset him. I don't speak German, and he lapses into it quite often when he's angry. He was composed again, though, by the time he returned to The Clouds later in the evening."

Wilson had been looking directly at each of us in turn as he spoke. Either he was telling the truth about not having been aware of Hermut's activities, or he was a damn good lawyer.

"Mr. Wilson," I said, "I didn't know you were friends with Hermut. Have you been friendly with him for long?"

Wilson directed intense eyes at me first before turning to his lawyer, who met his glance and nodded. Looking back at me again, Wilson sighed and just above a whisper, said, "We were lovers."

The walls of the room went silent. Even the corporal's pen had stopped scratching for the moment. I wasn't sure how to react, but Wilson's announcement definitely took me by surprise.

Mr. Williams came to our rescue. "I would like to take my client out of this room for a private discussion, if I may."

As they left, the inspector turned to the corporal and asked, "What does he mean?" The corporal gave an embarrassed shrug.

"They're gay," I answered, and watched the look on the inspector's face change from one of surprise to disgust. Because homosexuality is considered a disease or a scourge by many people in this country, I knew it would now be impossible for Wilson to receive an unbiased and sympathetic hearing, at least from this man. Mr. Williams had probably figured that out the moment Wilson dropped his bombshell and that's why he'd hustled his client out to counsel him as to what he should do next.

While we waited for them to return, I considered things. Now it was all beginning to fall into place. Wilson hadn't said so, but I assumed Hermut, being on such intimate terms with the owner, had key privileges to The Clouds. Mike's suggestion popped into my head—that we just needed to find out who had the key to the house in order to discover the person responsible for the crimes of that past week.

And it all made sense. Sarah would have known Hermut. If he was the one who called when Ned was in the shower, he could have easily talked her into accompanying him to the house that Sunday evening, where he then murdered her. Maybe Big Fly saw or heard something about Sarah he shouldn't have and was then also killed by Hermut. Or maybe Hermut asked someone else to do his dirty work. Since I had seen Pigface at his bar the night before the fishing trip, Hermut was most likely the one who hired the drug boys as hit men, in an attempt to get Al and me out of the picture. It was also probable Hermut had contacted Wilson earlier in the week and persuaded him to take me off the investigation.

What Hermut did to Angie may even have been his way of punishing me for not taking the hint to quit. When I thought about it, he had certainly been sneering at me the previous morning, although at the time I had the impression it was just his way of being funny. He actually had been thumbing his nose at me. Then there was that punch to my eye. Starting the fire and injuring Angie seemed more like acts of a desperate man, though, than someone trying to cover up a murder.

The inspector was called out of the room to take a phone call and, when he returned, it was to give me more bad news.

"De police on de mainland have discerned Mr. Landecker flew out of de country this morning. He left on a flight to Grenada. From there, he could have taken any number of international flights. The Grenada police are checking all de outbound passenger lists," he said, a bit deflated.

I couldn't believe my ears. Hermut had managed to slip away without the slightest trouble. It was as though the police had been helping him escape. He must have gone to Kingstown the day before to book his tickets. Hopefully, no matter where he managed to go, Interpol would be more successful than the Royal St. Vincent and the Grenadines Police Force had been in tracking him down. That is, unless he was now travelling under an assumed name.

Wilson and his lawyer came into the room. "Hermut skipped the country," I said. "They think he's already managed to fly out of Grenada."

Wilson seemed about ready to start crying. He looked at me and said, "Geoff, my lawyer has advised I say nothing further at this time, but I want to tell you again, personally, I had nothing to do with any of this. However, I do feel so very responsible for what has happened to you, and particularly to Angie, because of Hermut. My offer of this morning still stands. I would like to pay for all of Angie's medical expenses. Please don't turn me down on this. It's the least I can do, and I hope it will be one small way I can make everything up to you for what you've both suffered." Then after a pause, he added, "I've been so stupid, so stupid!" He covered his face with both hands and really did break down.

Mr. Williams patted Wilson on the shoulder then helped him sit back down at the table. He gestured I should leave. The inspector followed me out of the room and closed the door behind us.

"This is a mess," the inspector said when we were alone again. "It looks as though the culprit has managed to elude us." He shook his head.

My jaw dropped and I looked at the inspector in silent amazement. I wanted to point out that had Kydd not been incommunicado the night before, causing us to lose precious time, the culprit would never have left Bequia in the first place. But I had more important things on my mind than chastising the man for the force's complete incompetence.

"Inspector, now that we know who probably committed the murders and that I am no longer a suspect—I hope—am I free to leave the country? I don't want to go far, just to Barbados to be with

Angie while she's in the hospital. I'll come back whenever you need me to attend a hearing or an inquest or whatever happens next. I promise."

I felt confident he'd see his way to allowing me to travel again, knowing the things I now knew about him and how he had gone about his job the night before. I didn't want to play my trump card yet but was sure he wouldn't want the commissioner of police hearing from me at all.

"Okay," Kydd said, "but leave a phone number where we can reach you, just in case we need to ask you to return right away." He sounded officious and in charge once again, but I didn't care anymore. I was on my way to see Angie!

I said goodbye. The inspector turned his back on me and opened the door to the meeting room. As I was leaving the station, I heard him say, "I wonder if you gentlemen would find it in your hearts to donate money to my church . . ."

First I had to look for Al. I left the police station and headed down the road towards the Harbour. I was so elated at the thought of seeing my Ange again that I felt like I was walking on air!

And, boy, it was really turning into my lucky day. When I got to the main intersection of Port Elizabeth, I saw Al sashaying down the road towards me.

"Al, you're just the man I want to see!" I shouted. I walked over to him, grabbed his hand, and shook it. "I'll let you be the first to congratulate me, man! I'm free! I can fly to Barbados. I'm going to see Ange!"

"Great, Geoff! I'll fly you over later today. I have to go back there to pick up Melanie and some charter passengers, anyway." Then Al added, "I was on my way to the New York Bar just now to sit for a little while and watch the world walk by. Why don't you join me? Let me buy you a drink. I'm only having something soft since I have to fly later today, so no worries. Your pilot will be safe and courteous but not drunk. You can fill me in on everything that's happened."

"An excellent suggestion," I said with enthusiasm.

We walked down the road together the hundred yards or so and into the bar.

The usual group of Friday afternoon drinkers was already ensconced inside, although Mike wasn't yet among them. This being one of his regular social clubs, it was hard to believe he had something better to do at eleven-thirty on a Friday morning than drink at the New York Bar. Of course, like me, he had also been up all night but was probably the smarter one and still asleep on his boat.

Al and I took our drinks to the table outside and sat under the umbrella.

"Everything can be traced back to Hermut. But the bastard managed to escape."

"No kidding? Now tell me, that wasn't due to anything done by our illustrious police force, was it?"

"You're right; it wasn't due to anything they did, because they did nothing. What a waste of space and resources they are! And, I'm sorry to say, Celesta told me this morning her son has become one of them."

"Let's hope he's different from the rest. He should be, with Celesta as a mother. But the state this force is in, it won't provide him with any good role models, will it? They'd probably do well to hire Celesta to kick-ass the whole bunch of them into shape along with her son." We shook our heads at the idiocy of the situation.

We speculated about events until it was time to go.

When parting in the street, Al asked, "How long do you expect to be staying with Angie in Barbados?"

"They won't release her from the hospital for a few days. Until then, I guess."

"Well, don't forget, there's a full moon party at Henri-Alfred's house tomorrow night. Angie will probably be tired of you moping around her bedside by then, anyway, so you might as well come back here in the afternoon. Besides, I got a call this morning from Dimitri and Dejanari. They fly into Barbados tomorrow. I'm going over to bring them here, so you can fly back at the same time with us. It will be some party with D and D visiting!"

It would be. Dimitri and Dejanari Stephanopolus are Greeks who run a private sail charter business in the Aegean. They've been friends with Al and Suzie since they all met in the Mediterranean.

Dimitri and Dejanari have visited Bequia often over the years. And this couple definitely does like to party. It wouldn't surprise me if they had organized their visit to coincide with the upcoming full moon party. With all I had to celebrate, I'd have to make sure I paced myself that next night. They can be a bad influence and cause everyone else to get carried away along with them.

"Okay, you've convinced me. It will be good to see them again. I'll come back for that party tomorrow—that is, if Angie agrees."

"Great! See you at the airport, then, around three." He left me and danced down the main road into the centre of town, singing Trooper's *We're Here for a Good Time* to no one in particular.

That man certainly does dance to a different drummer and never ceases to amaze me. I stood there for a moment, shaking my head in wonder, then walked over to the wharf to get my car and drive back home. I was pleased with myself because as I passed Doris Fresh Food I thought to stop and buy some of those Belgian chocolates Angie loves so much. Hell, I was feeling so happy I even bought enough treats to dispense to her entire medical staff.

Chapter Ten

Al, Dimitri, Dejanari and I went directly to Moonhole after arriving at the Bequia airport on Saturday evening.

Henri-Alfred's house is at the top of a steep, winding, and fairly crooked set of stairs and hidden from the road by surrounding trees and bush. Perched on the side of a cliff, the house looks directly down on the Caribbean Sea to one side and, on the other, there's a sweeping view towards the Atlantic Ocean southeast of Bequia over a number of neighbouring islands. A constant breeze blows through the non-traditional open doors and windows. As a result, there are seldom any mosquitoes. Bonus!

In his ongoing remodelling efforts, Henri-Alfred has created some pretty interesting conversation areas in the house, but my favourite place to sit during a full moon party is always the flat roof, furnished with just a couple of lounge chairs and a ceiling of stars. After Henri-Alfred welcomed us at the entrance to his house, I poured a drink and went directly to the roof.

"I have a veritable United Nations in attendance at the party tonight," Henri-Alfred said on our way upstairs. "There's Norwegians, Germans, French, a couple of Italians, an Australian, and a South African, besides the usual assortment of Canadians, Americans, and British. The Hallidays are already here. They brought Su-

zie with them as well as the ice." I was off the hook. I'd actually forgotten my promise to supply it. "Mike's here, too. He sailed his boat
around and moored it in Adam's Bay."

We climbed the final set of stairs up to the roof—Henri-Alfred
called this his "stairway to heaven"—and found the Hallidays, Suzie,
and Mike already waiting for us. They'd thought to bring Ned along.
Suzie and Melanie took their turns hugging and fussing over me,
wanting to know all about Angie. Everyone greeted the Stephanopolouses, happy to see them back again on Bequia. Then they turned
to me for my full report on Angie's condition.

I walked into Angie's hospital room and was pleased to see my appearance had an immediate positive effect; her gloomy look disappeared and was replaced with a big smile. In spite of all the bandages, she was beginning to resemble the old Angie I loved so much.
Her voice was sounding better, as well.

"Oh, Geoffrey, I'm so happy to see you," she said, still croaking.

"No talking," I said as I kissed her with care, applying a soft
stroke to a small un-bandaged spot on her cheek. "The doctor told
me you're not to talk at all, or at least as little as possible. And this
time, for once in your life, you must do as we say."

Angie furrowed her brow. I knew how much she hated being told
what to do, so I laughed at her consternation then said in a whisper,
"Actually, I had to promise the doctor I wouldn't let you talk in exchange
for allowing me to spend the night with you." That brightened her up
and got her smiling again. "But," I waved one index finger at her, "no
matter how much you beg, there'll be no sex whatsoever." Holding up
both hands, I continued with my dramatics. "No, Mademoiselle, I don't
care what you say or do to entice me. Besides, spending the night with
you is really just my way of saving the expense of a hotel room."

She slapped at me for teasing her, then we both laughed. It
was so good to have my old Angie back again. I had felt helpless the
night before without her.

So, for the first part of my visit, I did all the talking, telling Angie everything I knew and what I'd recently learned of Hermut and Wilson, how Gus was faring, and all that had happened on Bequia since the fire.

But there's no stopping her when Angie is determined so, in spite of my promise to the doctor, over the next few hours she managed to whisper out the details of her ordeal. I would have preferred that she write it, but her right hand had been too badly injured to allow for holding a pen.

"Hermut came to the boathouse in the afternoon, shortly after two o'clock. I had just driven back from town and put away a few groceries before he knocked on the door. He was pleasant at first, said he was looking for you. He had something to tell you about the murders. When I told him you were still in St. Vincent, he suddenly seemed on the verge of hysterics. I thought that odd. He was certainly overreacting."

"Yeah, well he'd already done this to me." I pointed at my eye and accepted her fussing over me for a moment. "It's really nothing compared to what he did to you. Who knows what was going on in the guy's mind? You didn't know Hermut any better than I did, but I have heard he has a reputation of being a control freak, including in control of his emotions. Maybe when he discovered I wasn't home, and whatever his plans he had for me were defeated, he snapped."

"I think that's what happened. Maybe he decided then on kidnapping me instead."

"Either as a way of flushing me out when I went looking for you, or as punishment for having been in his way this past week?"

"I don't know, Geoffrey. He didn't explain anything to me, so I wasn't clear on his reasoning. By then any reasoning he might have had went haywire, anyway. He seemed desperate."

"That's what I thought happened. He became desperate."

"He forced me to write that note. I tried making it as cryptic as I could to warn you of trouble. Did you understand what I was telling you when you read it?"

"Ange, you know I'm a dolt when it comes to word puzzles of any kind. It seemed odd that you'd be going to a hen party, but I didn't clue into your real message. Sorry about that."

"Well, I should have considered you would take me literally." Angie reached for my hand. "You never were very good at reading between the lines. I was taking a chance you might be able to figure it out. I couldn't very well write 'Hermut is here and about to take me prisoner,' could I?"

"If only I had read the note to Mel. I'll bet she would have understood that something was wrong."

"No point in beating yourself up about that now. You likely wouldn't have found me, in any case. After I wrote the note, he taped my mouth and tied my hands behind my back. He was dragging me out to his car when Gus ran at us out of nowhere and started attacking Hermut. He ripped a pant leg."

We'd never trained Gus at all, but he'd always had a strong instinct to protect Angie.

"Hermut untied my hands and ordered me to get Gus under control. I was told to lock him up inside the house. Then Hermut put me into the boot of his car. He bound my legs together as well and closed me in."

The driveway entrance to our boathouse is fairly sheltered, so Hermut would have been able to do all this without being observed by any of our neighbours.

"Then he drove away, but I couldn't possibly have known where he was taking me. I did hear familiar noises along the way and knew we were driving through Port Elizabeth, but after that, I lost my bearings.

"When he stopped the car again, we were somewhere quiet. I guessed it was far away from the main part of the island, because it was at least fifteen minutes after driving through town before we stopped again. Hermut got out of the car and was gone for about five minutes. Then he came back. He was talking—to himself, I guessed; I don't think anyone else was there. He was ranting about something as he walked around in front of the car. It sounded like he was pacing back and forth, but it was all German he spoke and I didn't understand. The one word I do remember, because he kept repeating it, was *Geld*."

"Money," I said.

Angie looked puzzled. She was also appearing strained after having talked so much.

"Give your voice a rest, Ange. Let me talk for a while. I haven't told you yet—the Brethren found two suitcases full of US cash buried at The Clouds, close to where they found the clothes and gun the other day. I'll bet that was Hermut's money and he drove to the house so he could dig it up. When it wasn't where he'd left it, he became even crazier than before. It seems old Hermut may have been involved in more than just your kidnapping. He was probably hoping to retrieve this stash before Wilson arrived. No wonder the guy was in such a state."

"I think he kidnapped me before he knew the money was missing. So why was I kidnapped?"

"Probably as a way of getting back at me. Then knowing the money was gone just made it all the worse. At that point, he was more than capable of doing anything. Like we said, a desperate man."

"What did you and the Brethren do with the suitcases?"

"Well, reluctantly, we're going to turn all the money over to the police. The Brethren at least deserve a finder's fee, if not the whole amount. That money would set them up for the rest of their lives."

I'd said we were reluctant because instead of the money being used as evidence in a trial then burned afterwards, as is supposed to be done, we knew it would most likely end up in the general government coffers or, even worse, in someone's back pocket. Corruption can be insidious in this country.

I told Angie to rest again for a while before she continued her story. We had the whole night, after all.

When she resumed talking, Angie said, "I had figured out, by the time Hermut began to rant, that he must have taken me to The Clouds. This was confirmed when I heard another vehicle arrive. It sounded like a taxi. I heard a second man's voice, a local voice, so he was probably the driver. Then the vehicle drove away immediately and I heard Mr. Wilson calling hello to Hermut and Hermut answering. I tried kicking at the inside of the boot to signal Wilson, but Hermut must have parked his car too far away for me to be heard.

"I could tell from their short conversation before they entered the house that they were on friendly terms with each other. I heard what sounded like backslapping, you know, when friends hug each other? Hermut was composed by then, his speech back to normal. He told Wilson he had opened up the house in anticipation of his arrival."

"I thought he must have had a key."

"Yes. I realized it then as well. But I also thought it possible Wilson was in on everything that was happening. Getting his attention could have done me more harm than good, so I stopped trying and remained silent.

"Hermut and Wilson stayed inside the house. I didn't hear anything at all from them for about an hour, or maybe an hour and a half. Then Hermut came back to the car alone and drove away. I wasn't sure how long he drove around or where we went; I lost track of time. It was stifling in that boot. When the car finally stopped, Hermut came around to the back and opened the lid. He untied my legs, warned me not to do anything to try to escape, then helped me out. It was dark. We were back at our house again, but this time Hermut had parked out of sight behind the villa.

"He had our set of keys. The only way I could figure was he had pocketed the spare set when we were together earlier in the boat-house kitchen." We've always hung extra keys to both houses, rather foolishly I now realized, on a rack of hooks on the wall.

"Once we were inside the villa, Hermut retied my legs and left me lying on the kitchen floor while he went back out to the car. During the time he was gone, I noticed that the knot in the rope binding my wrists was loose. Hermut had been holding it while he was dragging me around, so he probably jiggled it. I decided to wait before attempting to struggle free. I didn't want to draw his attention to the fact there was a chance I might escape.

"Hermut returned carrying a jerry can he must have had with him in the car. I smelled petrol. He started pouring it all around." Angie gasped when telling me this.

"Catch your breath, love. Don't rush." The memory would have been horrible for her.

After a moment, she continued. "When I realized what he planned to do, I really began struggling with the loose knot. I was almost free of it when I heard barking at the back of the house. Hermut was startled by the noise, but then he also noticed me working to get my hands free. He struck the side of my head with the back of his hand. I presume I lost consciousness, either from the blow or the resulting hit my head took on the floor, because when I awoke, Gus was licking my face and whimpering. The house was already on fire, as far as I knew Hermut had left, and I can only surmise Gus must have chased him away."

Angie rested again, more to relax from the increased emotion than because of any strain to her voice. "I was finally able to free my hands; I took the tape off my mouth and untied my legs. By that time, the fire had spread, but the kitchen was still mainly filled with smoke. That caused both of us, Gus and me, to cough excessively."

I said, "We think it was probably Henry's vintage porn video collection that produced all that smoke." The man's love of porn was yet another reason to be angry with Henry.

Angie continued, saying, "Once I was mobile, it was all I could do to crawl out of the villa. I probably passed out again outside the back door, because I can't remember anything else after that, not until I regained consciousness later in the clinic."

"The Brethren found you lying further down the path between the two houses, close to the boathouse. Gus was by your side, also unconscious."

"Gus must have dragged me there, Geoffrey." She began crying, realizing, as I was beginning to as well, what Gus had helped her avoid.

I hugged Angie as best I could, and said, "It looks like our little wonder hound saved your life, Ange. If you had stayed in back of the house where you said you managed to crawl, you would have been lying right next to those two propane tanks that blew up."

Gus hadn't known he was doing anything heroic. He probably only had it in his mind to take Angie to the safest place in his world—the boathouse. And what he lacks in body size, he more than makes up for in heart.

"We are so fortunate to have that dog," Angie said.

She remained quiet for a short time, just thinking, then said, "Geoffrey, I don't know what was going on with Hermut, but it seemed there was more behind what he did to me last night than mere revenge. I had a feeling he hated me. It was an absolute and pure hatred, extremely deep seated. I can't explain it. He has no reason to hate me; he doesn't even know me." She had a puzzled look on her face.

"I don't know what it was, Ange. If it had been me he attacked, I could understand his hatred. I'm sure he's considered me a thorn in his side all week and was hoping to get rid of me altogether when he showed up at our door yesterday."

Angie squeezed her eyes as though trying to shut out recurring images running through her mind.

"But, no more talk now. I've heard enough and you look exhausted." I stroked her cheek with my hand and she opened her eyes again.

"I'll be all right, Geoffrey." But even having whispered everything, she'd talked too long and I could hear her voice was at an end. The doctor would not be happy with me in the morning. I hadn't kept my promise. But getting the story out had done her a lot of good, mentally. It had done both of us a lot of good, finally knowing the truth.

For the rest of that night, Angie slept while I sat in a chair by the bed and held her hand. The next morning she was forced to keep quiet and let me do all the talking while nurses and doctors bustled in and out of the room, so I used the opportunity to fill her in on my plans for our future, now that I had lost one property to manage but gained it back as a new property to own.

"Maybe when you're well we should consider getting away from Bequia for a while. Let's plan a real vacation. We deserve it. We've never gone anywhere together. I'd love to take you to Italy," I said. Other than the trip to Barbados to see Angie, I hadn't been away from Bequia since I'd arrived two years before. I was long overdue to get off island.

"Oh, Geoffrey, we could go to La Strada! And Venice!"

"Well, I can't guarantee the opera, but I'd love to be real tourists and take a gondola ride."

What I didn't dare mention was the serious possibility she might never sing again. It was something we would both have to face at a later date, but that future didn't warrant the slightest thought from either of us at that moment.

When I left Angie, she was in good spirits. The doctor had told us she would probably be released the following Monday and could go back home to Bequia.

"Geoff, you deserve another drink. Give me your glass," Henri-Alfred said. He began walking down the stairs, shouting back over his shoulder to everyone, "And don't forget there's lots of food. Come on down and help yourselves. Remember, we're all here cause we're not all there." He laughed as he continued his descent.

A few of the people who had been listening to me followed Henri-Alfred downstairs. Mike stayed, though, to tell me some of the other things about Hermut he'd heard around Lower Bay during the day.

"Now that he's departed the scene, tongues have suddenly loosened and are wagging frantically. And it seems no one can say anything good about the man, either."

It might have been fear of reprisal that kept everyone quiet while Hermut was still on the island, but I knew this is also the Bequia way. I've seen it happen before. No one seems to know the identity of a thief until he's caught and charged. Then, suddenly, everyone says they knew all along he was a bad guy and had been the one who committed the crime. So, you want to ask all of them, if you knew he was responsible, why didn't you warn someone before more damage was done? Or maybe it's the case that Bequia people want everyone else to think they are always right and have all the answers, albeit only after the fact. It's another one of those Bequia oddities, as far as I can tell.

"Now rumours are rife Mr. Landecker was involved in everything, from a prostitution ring, illegal gambling and porn movies to government kick-backs," Mike said. "I guess that the truest rumour, though, is that he's been the king-pin of an international drug-smuggling organization."

"That makes sense," Al said, out of the darkness. I'd forgotten he was there. Looking over at him, I caught the slight nod, agreeing we continue our silence about the fishing trip.

"Now that I think of it, Mike, Hermut was probably dispensing crack from behind his bar," I said. "While we were sitting at the table the other evening, all those people kept coming in for quick drinks then left immediately. They must have been buying crack as well as drinks. You even said there had likely been a crack shipment recently."

"Yeah, too right, but I didn't know when I said it exactly how close we were to the source of the crack. I guess my ability to stay on top of local gossip must be slipping if that obvious fact managed to escape me." Mike looked a little crestfallen.

Al said, quipping, "You'd better watch out, Mike; those ladies won't be inviting you to join them for lunch any longer if you can't keep them better informed."

"Well, whatever Hermut was involved in here," I said, "let's hope he's gone now, and for good. And not only for our good, either, but for the good of Bequia. I doubt it ever occurred to him to groom someone else as a replacement, so I hope his exit from the scene finally kills the island crack business, or at least throws a big wrench into it for a while."

Everyone agreed—stopping the availability of crack cocaine on Bequia could only be a good thing, although with the amount of money involved in its sale and transport, we all knew it would only be a matter of time before someone else stepped in and took over.

Doc said, "Something's not clear to me, Geoff. If Hermut was seeking revenge, why did he try to burn down the villa and not the boathouse where you actually live?"

"I don't know the answer. Maybe he thought I owned the villa as well as the boathouse. I guess we'll never know now, will we?"

The rest of my friends all went downstairs to join the other guests at the food table.

I stayed up on the roof for a few more minutes, on my own, so I could have a good look at that sky filled with billions of stars. A bounteous full moon was beginning to make its appearance. We still hadn't had any rain yet, but it generally arrives with a full moon. I noticed the wind was picking up; we were in for a change in weather. It didn't look like we'd get rain that night, though. Bequia needed some moisture; it was starting to look a little too dry. The tourists wouldn't be happy if the crystal-clear blue skies and dry weather they were enjoying didn't continue through their entire vacation. But into every life a little rain must fall, otherwise all the gardens on the island would wither, making a property manager's job hell. I was seriously hoping for lots of rain.

While standing there, alone, I allowed the island breeze to blow the remaining cobwebs out of my head and I tried, tried very hard, to think of nothing at all.

Early Sunday morning, the group of us met on the beach in front of Mac's. *OneLove* was waiting; the Hallidays, Mike, and Ned were already on board when I climbed the steps to join them. Mr. Wilson was walking along the beach towards the boat, clutching what must have been the urn containing Sarah's ashes. Al, Suzie, Dimitri, and Dejanari followed closely behind. Once everyone was on the boat, the captain took us out of the Harbour.

Wilson hadn't wanted a religious ceremony, so, when we were a short distance away from the island, he simply scattered Sarah's ashes on the water then turned to face all of us.

"I want to thank you for everything you've done this week. And I want to apologize. I'm as shocked as all of you—probably more," he said, with hesitation, "by what has happened on Bequia and what Hermut has done. I blame myself completely for this. If I hadn't been so secretive about being gay then none of this would have—nothing might— " He collected his thoughts. "If it had been known on Bequia that Hermut was gay, and if our relationship was revealed sooner, things would have been far different. I feel relieved now my secret is out in the open, but people shouldn't have died or been injured to protect my reputation. If I'd only known— " Wilson lost his composure altogether and started crying.

As a way of drawing attention from Wilson, and allowing the man a moment to contain himself, Melanie stood up and said, "Most of us didn't know Sarah at all, but we did know she was loved by her husband and— " Her voice trailed off as she glanced over at Ned. She cleared her throat and continued. "Sarah was the victim of a heinous crime. No one's life should come to an end at such a young age. We all mourn her and, no matter what our religious beliefs, we trust that she's gone on to a better place."

When Melanie sat down, the captain turned the boat around and we headed back towards Bequia.

Wilson came over and asked me to move to one side of the boat so we could talk in private. "Geoff, it's you especially I want to thank. I now realize you were in grave danger this week, and Angie has been badly injured as a result of my stupidity. I don't think it possible I could ever offer compensation to either of you that will make up for what you both have suffered." He paused a moment then said, "I should tell you I've decided to leave Bequia for good. I'm going to put The Clouds up for sale."

Suddenly, my property management clients were dropping like flies sprayed with Baygon.

"I'm sorry to hear that, Mr. Wilson, but I can understand how you must feel about the island and why you wouldn't want to come back here again. If I hear of anyone who's interested in buying your place, I'll let you know."

As he was turning away, I said, "There is just one thing I'd like you to explain, Mr. Wilson, and this might be a bit delicate, but it's been bothering me. I hope you don't mind my asking." I hesitated before continuing. "Hermut had this reputation on Bequia for preferring teenaged girls. Was he bisexual?"

"No. Hermut started that rumour as a way to cover his homosexuality. He's a misogynist."

Oh, so now I understood—Hermut hated women. That accounted for the extreme sense of hatred Angie said she'd detected. It also explained the misconception everyone had about him. He'd been able to manufacture a plausible personality for himself in order to mask the truth.

"Hermut was aware of the local attitude towards gays," Wilson said. "We both managed to keep our relationship completely secret even from Sarah, for a while, but she walked in on us one day at The Clouds. We didn't know she'd caught an earlier boat home from St. Vincent so hadn't expected her to return to the house that afternoon. Understandably, she went crazy when she discovered the truth about me. She immediately went out and started that silly affair with Big Fly as a way of punishing me."

Wilson's confession proved that the Bequia rumour-mongers had had it all wrong—the Wilsons' separation was a result of his bad behaviour, not hers.

"Do you think Sarah came back to Bequia this time to blackmail you, then?"

I hoped I wasn't pushing him for more information than I had a right to know, but I really needed to clear things up, if only to straighten it all out in my own mind.

"No, Sarah was attempting to blackmail Hermut, not me. I think she knew he was involved in some very big money that was illegal. He told me Thursday night she had been threatening to tell me he was up to something and using my house, and that she would report it all to the authorities in such a way as to implicate me if he were caught. He, of course, denied he was doing anything illegal at all and, foolishly, I believed him. He also said he'd had nothing to do with Sarah's murder. I believed that, too. I loved him. What more can I say?"

It was hard to imagine, Wilson loving Hermut, but they do say love is blind. I would have to add that, in this case, love was also deaf, dumb, and stupid.

I paused for a moment before continuing. "I know I said I only wanted you to explain one thing to me, Mr. Wilson, and you've been good about answering my other questions, but there is one last point I still don't understand."

"Go ahead, Geoff. What's that?"

"Why was Big Fly so insistent I tell you to get an AIDS test?"

He gazed off at the horizon then looked at me and said, "That's because Hermut had been sleeping with Big Fly as well as with me. In fact, Hermut was probably the one who was carrying the virus in the first place, only he didn't bother to tell me that news. Before I had dinner with you on Thursday night, I saw Hermut. He was waiting for me at The Clouds. He announced then he had taken another lover, a young boy. At the time, I thought I must have fallen out of favour with him, maybe I was too old, but now I know it was probably the case that my house was of no further use, so he was discarding me as well. Whatever the reason, he was leaving me for this young man. He didn't tell me the name at the time; he also didn't bother telling me that the same young man was the other body you found in my pool. Each thing Hermut said was just another big lie. I guessed who Hermut's new lover was, though, as soon as you told me that Big Fly insisted I get an AIDS test. No doubt Big Fly had been humouring Hermut in exchange for money. He was a poor boy and easily influenced by any amount of cash. Little did Big Fly know that when all was said and done he'd end up with AIDS, and," Wilson shook his head, "murdered."

"Did Big Fly tell Hermut he'd informed Sarah, or maybe threatened to tell you?"

"Who knows? Hermut didn't tell me anything. He was using Big Fly, just like he'd used me. Like he used everyone. Since I didn't know Hermut had already killed Big Fly, I figured the real reason Hermut said he was leaving was because he'd actually fallen out of love with me, plain and simple. I couldn't admit though he was *never* in love with me. I'm still having trouble believing that."

I kept my silence and let him continue.

"Soon after I returned from dinner on Thursday, Hermut arrived at my house again, saying he still wanted to be friends. He must have come back after he started the fire. I confronted him then with what I'd figured out from our conversation. He denied it all, but became angry and agitated with me. I assume he did so because he was still lying about everything, and this was his means of defence. Now, knowing about the fire and Angie, it was probably because he was worked up over what he'd done. At one point during the night, he even tried to twist things around and put the blame on me, saying I had caused him to turn to Big Fly in the first place. Again, it was all lies to distract me from what had really happened. I let him sweet-talk me one last time, though, thinking I might be able to work things out and win him back again. We even slept together that night, but he left early in the morning, and I never saw him again."

He stopped talking then and looked as though maybe he'd said more than he'd wanted me to know. With a simple "excuse me, Geoff," he walked away from me and over to Ned Watson to introduce himself.

We didn't speak to each other again that day.

OneLove pulled up on the beach and we all got off the catamaran. Mr. Wilson thanked everyone one more time then walked down the beach, accompanied by Ned. While we watched them disappear, someone, and it might have been Mike, said, "Hmmmmmm," under his breath. We all exchanged inquiring glances, but nothing else was said about that.

"Okay, gang," Melanie said, "I have pancakes ready to go at our house. Is anyone hungry?"

"What is it about a funeral at sea that gets me to salivating?" Al said, laughing.

"Al!" Suzie snapped, reeling him back in line behind her and the Stephanopolouses. "We will meet you there, Melanie. Thank you," she said over her shoulder.

"I don't know about you, mate, but I'm half starved," Mike said.

"Come on, I'll drive," I said, also looking forward to a good feed of pancakes. Al had been partly right. It's amazing how even a short boat ride on open water can pique the appetite.

I buckled my seatbelt and waited as Al made his final checks before taking off. It was Sunday afternoon and we were flying back to Barbados so I could spend another night with Angie then accompany her home to Bequia on Monday. Al's B-Islander is too noisy to allow for conversation, so I settled in for an hour alone with my thoughts, or even, I hoped, to catch up on some much-needed sleep.

But I did have a lot to think about. Life on Bequia had changed in a sudden and drastic way, for both Angie and me. My business would have to be reorganized and I'd probably need a few new clients to keep enough money coming in to allow us to continue living in the manner to which we'd become accustomed. We now owned a house that would provide us with a good rental income one day, but first it required extensive rebuilding, and construction never proceeds fast, or cheap, on Bequia.

Angie had a long recovery ahead of her if she were to sing again—that is, if she ever completely recovered. The doctors wouldn't give us any answers yet. We had to wait and see.

I also could no longer count on a prospective payoff from my former friends, but then at least I didn't feel guilty anymore about that past episode in my life.

And Gus was going to be a mangy dog once again until his hair grew back.

I hoped one thing hadn't changed as a result of that past week: my relationship with Angie, the one person in my entire life I hold dear. It hit me like a wallop to my chest how deeply I loved her. The week's events actually intensified that love and really solidified us as a couple. I don't know what I would have done if I'd lost her.

Al taxied down the runway and we were soon in the air, flying eastward, following the southern shore of the island. I took in everything on the ground below, mentally pointing out houses and sites I recognized. As we passed over Friendship Bay, I was amazed, yet again, by the brilliant-blue tropical water, the golden-sand beach. I never tire of seeing that sight. I don't think I could ever be bored with it.

Then it struck me: Bequia really is a very special place, unlike anywhere else I'd ever lived. Even with what had happened to

Angie and me that past week, and how it had rearranged our lives, I couldn't imagine living anywhere else. The climate is great, year round. We normally lead a relatively stress-free existence, that past week aside, and live casually in a wardrobe of assorted shorts and T-shirts. We don't punch a time clock. There are many kind, decent people, and we have true, and fierce-loyal, friends. I was fortunate to have learned who those real friends are and that I can depend on them to come through whenever I need them most.

And, even with our recent setbacks, it would still be possible for me to rebuild my property management business, or start something altogether new if I wanted, for that matter; opportunities are definitely here. I've discovered the best part of living on Bequia is that people are allowed the option of being responsible for, and in control of, their own lives. I love that feeling of freedom.

Besides all that, Angie and I have each other, and we both have Gus. Yeah, yeah! All pretty mushy stuff, but what more could anyone ask for, or want, out of life?

What I especially hoped, though, was that Bequia would return once again to being the island where nothing ever happens. I could stand a little boring normalcy in my life. I'd discovered I wasn't able to handle too much excitement any more. Maybe it's a sign of age.

I looked through the windscreen. Ahead of us, out of sight, was Barbados. Thunderclouds had been gathering in that direction all morning. The plane was now out over the open ocean, past the tip of the island, so I turned my head to look out the side window, taking one last glance under the wing at Bequia.

I'll be back, I promised, watching the island disappear into the clouds.

Acknowledgements

Thanks to a great team – editing by Rachel Small, original print design by Jenny Ryan, and ebook formatting, listing and redesign of this second print edition by Regina McCreary, Human Powered Design.

You all make my words and stories look perfect!

And thanks to Dennis and the cats for keeping me grounded.

Susan M. Toy has been a bookseller,
an award-winning sales rep for publishers,
an author impresario, a consultant and a writer,
and is now a publisher.

She shares her time between a trailer in Canada
and a house, with four cats in the yard, on
the Caribbean island of Bequia.

For more information about **Susan M. Toy**
and her writing, please see:
https://islandeditions.wordpress.com

Printed in Great Britain
by Amazon

29029225R00108